All I Ever Wanted

STACY KRISTEN

Contents

All I Ever Wanted

Kelsie and Reese have been friends since high school. But for Reese, his biggest regret is letting Kelsie walk away without telling her his true feelings. But now Kelsie's back and he has one last shot at happiness. But will Kelsie feel the same way? Will there be a Christmas miracle?

*This is dedicated to my husband.
Thanks for everything babe.*

Chapter 1

FOXTAIL RIDGE

KELSIE

"Cheers, Sis!" I exclaim, holding up my beer. "To the future. May it be merry and bright. And the best thing that ever happened!"

"Cheers!" my sister Abbie cries happily, clinking her bottle against mine. I smile and gulp down more of my beer.

Tonight, we're celebrating my move back to Foxtail Ridge and my purchase of the old Johnson place up on the mountain. It was a bed and breakfast previously, but closed when the owners decided to up and sell. But the place never sold. It sat on the market for years, until they finally gave up and let the place just fall into disrepair, which is really sad. But that's not the end of the story; it's only the beginning. That's where I come in. I needed a change from my monotonous desk job in Denver, so I scraped together my meager savings and put a down payment on the old place. Now, I no longer have to commute and do the daily grind. Instead, I'll be living at the B&B, working to get the place cleaned up and ready to operate again. Abs volunteered to help me get everything set up, while she works from home as an editorial consultant. Which is fine by me, because I can use all the help I can get. From now on, I'll be serving my guests instead of my stuffy old boss. And I can't wait. Being my own boss will be challenging, but I'm up for it. And with Abbie's help, I'm sure I can make a go of it. She can be a bit of a diva, but I'm glad she's my sister and that I have her help.

Taking another swig of my beer, I look around. The local bar and grill, Sam's Place, is packed tonight. Hell, even the bar is jammed with people. Looks like we're not the only ones celebrating tonight, I muse.

"Ready to order?" Abbie asks, snapping me out of my reverie.

"Sure," I reply.

"I have a feeling if we don't order soon, it will take forever to get our food."

"Good point."

As soon as we got here, we snagged a booth in the back and ordered our beers. But now, we need food. I order a cheeseburger and Abbie orders a veggie wrap. *I know.* We're like night and day. That's what makes us so awesome.

While we wait, Abbie gets bored and looks at her phone and I do the same. But I grow bored quickly, so I decide to people watch instead. At first, I don't see anything exciting, just people going about their evenings, letting off a little steam on a Friday night. But then my eyes land on *him*, sitting at the bar, nursing a beer. *Reese Wilson.* I'm actually surprised to see him here tonight. He usually avoids crowds like they're the plague, giving them a wide berth.

Here's the thing about my old friend Reese. We're both locals; we both grew up in Foxtail Ridge, a small mountain town in Colorado. And we're both single. The difference between us? I just moved back. He never left. And not to mention he has all the town's single ladies chasing after him. Don't get me wrong, I went on a few dates when I lived in Denver, but no one really sparked my interest. Reese, on the other hand, can't keep women from chasing him. It's constant: women approach him all the time, flirting with him. They make googly eyes, smile and fake laugh, and touch him without asking, all trying to get with him. Except, no ladies ever do. He shuts them down. *Every. Single. Time.* He's never interested. *Wash, rinse, repeat.* But tonight, he looks miserable. He's slumped over the bar, nursing his beer, staring into the bottle like it has all the answers of the universe.

Oh, Reese, you poor man. Your life must be so hard I muse, making myself almost snort. Yeah, right!

My thoughts are interrupted by the arrival of our food. The smell alone has me salivating and my thoughts of Reese vanish quickly. I'm starving and ready to fill my empty belly.

"Ugg, that smells *so* good," Abbie says, smiling.

I smile and give her a pointed look. "Ready to come back to the dark side?

"Nope. I'm sticking to it. Vegetarian for life."

I shrug. "Your loss."

"Not really, but *okay*," she chirps back, laughing and smiling, giving me a silly face.

I return her smile and we both dig into our food. As I eat, I sneak glances at Reese, still at the bar. When I peek again, he has a fresh beer this time and he doesn't look so dejected. I wonder what made him so melancholy? I'm about to ponder that very question, when Abbie pushes her plate away and leans back, resting her back against the cushion, her hands over her tummy.

"I'm stuffed," she says, reaching for her purse.

"Ugg, me too," I sigh, pushing my plate away. I glance at

the bar again, looking for Reese, but he's no longer sitting at the bar. Looking around, I spot his tall frame headed toward the door.

"Earth to Kelsie," my sister says, interrupting my thoughts.

"What?" I say absently. I was so into watching Reese, that I didn't even register what she was saying.

"Ready to go?"

"Sure."

We pay and leave, heading into the parking lot. I'm hoping to spot Reese, but he's already gone, his heavy-duty work truck nowhere to be found.

I climb into the passenger seat, and Abbie drives us back to the B&B. My thoughts drift to what lays ahead—all the things I need to do to get my dream up and running. As one thought leads to another, my mind latches onto who else could help me with said dream—Reese Wilson, resident handyman extraordinaire.

Chapter 2

I finally got the keys and it's our first day at the old Johnson place. It's late Autumn and a crisp breeze gently blows, scattering leaves onto the ground. As we stand on the front porch, I take in the broken shutters and dirty panes of glass. I hope I haven't bit off more than I can chew.

"Ready?"

"Ready," Abs replies, eager to step inside. It gets chilly in a hurry up here.

Unlocking the front door, I swing it open and step inside, Abs on my heels. We're met with dust, cobwebs, and—

"What was that?!" I scream, jumping up and down. "Something just ran across my foot!" I yelp, stamping my feet.

I absolutely hate creepy critters and bugs. But whatever ran across my feet was not a spider. It was *way* too big for that.

"What? Where?" Abbie shrieks, the tone of her voice rising an octave. She's freaked out, too.

"I don't know," I say, breathing heavily. "But whatever it was, it was furry and in a hurry."

She looks around, hugging her arms to her body. All I can

see is dust. The stuff is everywhere, coating every surface. And from the looks of it, something has disturbed the dust. *But what was it?*

"I don't see anything else. Let's do a walk through, to see where we want to start. The place needs a thorough cleaning, from top to bottom."

"Are you sure you want to do that?" Abs asks me.

"Have to start somewhere," I say, a bit grim-faced.

Heading toward the stairs, I take each step slowly, gripping the wooden balustrade making sure I don't encounter anything else. Once we both reach the top, we roam about, taking stock of the bedrooms. Surprisingly—there's actually quite a bit of furniture left that is in usable shape.

"Well, what do you think about the furniture?" I ask.

"Even though it's old, I like it. It's rustic. And charming."

"Same. It just needs a good dose of old-fashioned elbow grease to clean it, then a new coat of paint."

"It sure does," she replies, smiling. "But have no fear, the Marsh sisters are on the job," she jokes, holding up her arms, patting her biceps.

I laugh lightly. My sister makes me smile. "Let's head downstairs to the kitchen. See what we're dealing with."

She nods, and I follow her down the stairs, walking to the back of the house. This is my happy place. I can't wait to cook and bake in this very kitchen for all my guests. It's going to be magical.

"Does anything even work?" Abs asks, opening the refrigerator door, peering inside.

"That's the million dollar question."

Swinging the oven door open, I peer inside, to see what kind of mess may be lurking. But surprisingly, it's clean and only a little dusty. Just like the rest of the place.

She snorts and tries the tap. Just then, the pipes rattle and rust-colored water slowly starts to sputter out. After a few seconds, the water runs clear again. At least we know something works.

Looking around the kitchen, I marvel at all the cabinets and counter space. Once we clean up the place, I'm going to enjoy filling the cabinets with all my cooking and baking paraphernalia. Even if it needs a complete overhaul. I'll just pretend it's vintage and it's cool. But eventually, the kitchen will need to be renovated.

Abbie looks at me, her eyes lighting up. "What are you going to name the place?"

Propping a hip against the counter, I ponder, totally faking her out. I already know what I'm naming the place. "Reindeer Inn!" I say excitedly, practically grinning from ear to ear.

"Oh my word, Kels! That's perfect!" she says happily.

"It is!" I tell her, saving the best part for last. "And it's going to be Christmas themed. Every room decorated with holiday cheer."

"I love it. It's a great idea!" she replies, her eyes almost twinkling.

"I knew you'd love it. You love Christmas as much as I do!"

"I do!"

Not only does Abs love Christmas, but I love it, too. To say I have a thing for Christmas is a *huge* understatement.

"I want to keep the feel of the place, just make it charming and full of Christmas spirit. All year long."

"It's going to be a destination, for sure."

I nod, agreeing. That is exactly what I want.

Since B&Bs are a dime a dozen in these parts, I need to make this place stand out from the rest. And a Christmas theme year around should do the trick. No matter what time of year it is, it's always going to be Christmas at The Reindeer Inn B&B.

What can I say? My sister and I *really* love Christmas. This way, I get to stay in the holiday spirit all year long. *Win-win.*

* * *

The next day Abs and I arrive at the B&B, supplies in tow.

"Do you think we brought enough cleaning supplies?" Abbie asks behind me, as she lugs three bags of stuff up the front steps.

"I hope so. I don't want to waste time going back down the mountain to get more," I tell her, hefting the rest of the cleaning supplies, including a broom and a mop.

Sitting everything on the front porch, I pull the key out and swing the door open wide. And right as I do, a raccoon shoots out the front door, right between my legs. I jump and let out a scream.

"Aaaagggggghhh!" I yell, stumbling backwards, bumping into Abbie.

My hand flies to my chest, my heart thumping rapidly. I suck in a few deep breaths, trying to calm down.

Abs stumbles and catches herself on the porch railing.

"What the heck was that?"

Looking over my shoulder, I see a raccoon waddling off toward the tree line.

"That was a raccoon. And I think he's been using the place as his home," I say, chuckling.

"Well," Abbie says, pausing. "No free rent. We need to find out where he got in and fix it."

"Agreed. He can stay on the property, but not in the house."

"Now that's out of the way, let's get started."

Abs and I trudge in, weighted down with so many cleaning supplies, we could clean a small mansion. Even though it seems like overkill, we have a lot of space to clean and the newly minted Reindeer Inn needs a thorough cleaning from top to bottom.

"Let's start upstairs," I tell Abs. "Sound good?"

"Mmm, hmm," she replies, following me up the stairs.

As we walk around the second story landing, I pick a room. Doesn't matter where we start, just that we do.

Pressing the light switch, the bulb flickers on, lighting up the space. And the dust. That's one thing we made sure to do after we were here yesterday, was to get the electricity turned on. Now we're back to get things cleaned up. And check to see if the kitchen appliances even work.

"Ready?" I ask.

"Ready as I'm ever going to be," Abs says, flipping open the music app on her phone. "Gotta have music."

I smile and push up my sleeves, ready to begin. I start by opening the windows, airing the place out. Then, I sweep every room and wipe down the furniture, while Abs fills the mop bucket with water and soap and mops behind me. The place is looking better already.

"What next?" she asks me.

"Bathrooms?"

"Yuck. Leave them for last. Let's clean everything first."

"Okay. Upstairs first, then we'll move to the first floor."

It ends up taking us the rest of the day to get everything clean. By the end, we're both tired and hungry.

"Let's go get something to eat."

"Now you're talking," Abs says heading to the front door. Stopping abruptly, I almost run into her back.

"Gee, Abs. Do you need brake lights?"

She tsks. "What about the raccoon? Maybe we should investigate and find out where he got in."

I sober instantly. "Oh my, yes. We need to find that entry point. Probably a good idea to do that before we leave."

"Yeah, cuz I totally don't want to have to re-clean everything we've done today."

"If that happened, I'd be so pissed."

"I'll take the second floor, and you take the first. I'll bet we can find it."

"Okay. Holler if you find it," I tell her.

"Will do," she says, walking upstairs.

I go through every single room and check all the windows and doors. No gaps. *Where could the raccoon have gotten in?*

"Found it!" Abs, hollers.

I race up the stairs. "Where?!" I holler, trying to find her. "Where are you?"

"Over here!"

I find her in one of the closets. "You've got to be kidding me."

"Nope. Not even a little bit," she says, pointing upwards. There's a hole, leading straight into the attic.

"Wow," I say, peering upwards. "We're going to have to plug it with something."

"With what?" Abs asks me.

I ponder a few seconds, when all of the sudden the lightbulb comes on in my head. "We have cardboard boxes. Maybe use one of those?"

"Hey, that could work. For now, at least."

"Okay, let me go get it. Be right back."

I head downstairs to get a cardboard box out of my SUV, and as I'm shutting the door, I hear the crunching of gravel and rock under vehicle tires. Someone is here, obvs. But who could it be? No one knows we're here. Whipping around, I put my hand up to shade my eyes. And what I see surprises me, as it's the last person I expected to see: Reese Wilson in his big, oversized heavy-duty work truck.

He pulls up next to my SUV and puts his truck in park. He rolls down his window, but doesn't get out. "Hey, I heard someone had bought the old Johnson place. Figured I'd come check it out."

I'm still shading my eyes from the sun. "Hey, Reese. How's it going? And you heard right."

"So you moved back and bought the old place. Nice to see the place is no longer sitting empty."

"Nope. I'll be opening it as a B&B again."

"By yourself? All the way up here?" he asks, curious.

"My sister Abbie is helping, but once I get it up and running, it'll be me and one other person, whenever I hire them."

"That's great. It'll be neat to have the old place up and running again."

"Sure will. I hope to have the Reindeer Inn open by Christmas."

"Well, now," he says, nodding at the old place. "By the looks of it, you're gonna need some help," he says, smiling, his dimples appearing.

I smile right back. "I'll most definitely need some help. I was actually about to give you a call this evening. Once I figured out everything that needed done."

Sneaky man. He totally knew what he was doing coming up here. But I was going to call him anyway, so I forgive him. Sigh...small towns. Everyone knows everyone else's business.

"In that case, I can take a look around. If you have time," he says, getting out of his truck.

As he steps down, I have to look up. Reese is 6 foot 3 inches of pure man, corded muscles from head to toe. You can tell he works with his hands, as he's in amazing shape.

He catches me looking and just gives me one of his trademark smiles with dimples again. "Head inside?"

"Yes," I say, turning on my heel.

He follows me inside and looks around, surveying the place, measuring it up, seeing what he needs to do to make the place livable again.

"I'm going to take this upstairs," I tell him, holding up the box.

He nods and continues to look around.

Taking the stairs one at a time, I tuck the box under my arm. And then it hits me—I probably look like total shit, because I'm dusty and dirty from cleaning all day. *Well, too late now.* If Reese saw it, he didn't let on. Bless the man.

"There you are. I thought you'd gotten lost. Did I hear you talking on the phone?" she asks me, taking the box from my hands.

"Talking, yes. Phone, no."

"Huh?" she asks, tearing off a flap of the box to cover the hole.

"Reese stopped by. Said he'd heard someone had bought the place. Guess he was curious to see who that was."

"Cat's out of the bag now. But who cares?! The more people talk, the more buzz it generates," she says, cramming the box into the hole. "There. I think I got it. It should work, for now."

I look up at the hole, the box covering it. "Works for me. Reese can fix it, if he's up for fixing this old place."

"Sure am," Reese says from the doorway, making us both jump.

Abbie eyeballs him. "Reese."

"Abbie," he says back.

He just smiles at her, turning on the charm, his dimples making an appearance again.

I look into his deep blue eyes. "You're hired," I say, laughing softly.

"All right, then. I'll draw up the paperwork tonight. Start on Monday?"

"Yes, Monday will work. I'll be moving in this weekend."

"See you both Monday then," he says, heading out.

Heaven help me. I just hired the most eligible bachelor in town. And he's already turning on the charm. Too bad he's an old friend and not someone I would even remotely think about dating.

Reese

It's perfect timing when I pull up to the old Johnson place. Kelsie, an old friend from high school, is bent over, ass in the air. She reaches for something in the back end of her SUV, pulling out a box. But that's not where my focus is. Nope. It's on the globes of her ass. And what a mighty fine ass it is. The thought makes me smile, even though I probably shouldn't be thinking about my old friend that way. She was never just my friend, but she doesn't know that. Here's the thing about us: we're old friends who spent most of our time together during high school. Some even said we were glued at the hip. We weren't, obviously, but we were each other's rock through all the ups and downs of growing up in a small town. We had each other's back.

After she graduated, she went off to college while I stayed in Foxtail Ridge. While she was busy getting her degree, I was busy taking over my Dad's home improvement business. I learned the ropes and expanded it, making it even more successful and profitable than it was before. And that's saying something, since my Dad was constantly busy when I was growing up. But the difference between then and now is that I have several crews who do most of the work. Don't get me wrong, I still do my fair share. But in addition to the hands-on labor, I also oversee every aspect of the business. Unfortunately, as Kels and I chased our dreams, we drifted apart. Then when she settled in Denver, instead of moving back to Foxtail Ridge, we drifted apart even further. But I never forgot the good times we had together. And my attraction to her has never waned. But she doesn't know the last part; the part where I've been secretly pining away for her since high school.

Chapter 3

"We should have asked for help," Abs grunts, as we maneuver my mattress through the door and up the stairs.

I'm finally moving in. And conveniently, our parents are on vacation or they would have helped.

"You're probably right. But it's too late now," I tell her.

"Are you sure you don't want to call and ask for help?" she mumbles.

"Not really. And besides, we're almost done," I tell her matter-of-factly.

She sighs and follows me up the stairs. I could have asked for help, but my sister and I are pretty independent. Besides, I don't have that much to move anyway, since I lived in a studio apartment in Denver. There's no need for our parents to help us move. They're getting up there in age and they don't need to be moving furniture or boxes. I can take care of it myself. With Abbie's help, of course.

After we've unloaded the last of my things, I call out to Abs. "I'm going to take the moving van back. Follow me?"

"Sure. Just give me a minute."

"Okay. Don't take too long," I holler up the stairs.

A few minutes later, she walks down the stairs, looking refreshed. Tucking my hair behind my ear, I probably should have cleaned up, too. But we need to get the moving van back before closing time.

"Ready?" I ask, grabbing my coat.

"Yep." She already has hers on.

I grab my purse and we walk out together. I get into the moving van and start it up, and Abs does the same to her SUV. It's time to take this thing back.

Later that night, I work on unpacking my stuff, when Abs walks in and sits on my bed.

"Almost done?"

I nod, putting away my clothes. "I really want to get this done, then start unpacking the kitchen. I also need to start ordering items for the B&B. Like a professional espresso machine. And lots of other goodies, such as linens and towels, soap and shampoo. And not to mention toilet paper and tissues. I also need to start looking for décor for each room, too."

Out of the corner of my eye, I see her nod in agreement. "Do you want to start unpacking the kitchen items?"

That seems to break her out of her funk. "Sure. I could use a change of pace," she replies. Getting off my bed, I see her walk out and head down the hall, toward the stairway.

I finish unpacking most of my stuff and head downstairs to help Abs. I'm tired, but there's so much more to be done, so I push on. As I step into the kitchen, I hear music playing, Abs dancing along to the music. It makes me smile.

Oh, Abs. Never change.

· · ·

By the time the clock strikes midnight, we've gotten almost all the kitchen stuff unpacked and put away, with only a few items left that I don't know where to put. But I'll find a place for them, eventually.

"Let's call it a night," I say, yawning.

She yawns back. "I'm so tired, I think I could sleep for a week."

"Me, too. Stay the night? There's no need to drive back down the mountain tonight."

"Sure," she replies, hiding a yawn behind her hand.

We climb the stairs and both fall onto my bed, tired beyond belief.

The next morning, I wake up bright and early thanks to the sun pouring into the windows. Note to self: need curtains. Smiling in spite of the brain-piercing rays, I throw back the covers and slide my feet into my faux fleece-lined slippers and grab my soft, fuzzy white robe. Pulling it on, I pull it closed and belt it snugly. The old place gets a little bit chilly in the mornings. Another note to self: get the heater checked, too. Stretching, I feel rested and ready to take on the day.

Quietly as possible, I creep from the bedroom and head downstairs to the kitchen. *I need coffee. Stat.*

As I make my way downstairs, I try to keep as quiet as possible. Abbie is *so* not a morning person. It's best to let her sleep just a little bit longer. As soon as I step into the kitchen, the first thing I do is start the coffee maker. As it sputters to life, I grab a white chocolate raspberry scone I made and take a big bite, enjoying my little lump of baked goodness.

Leaning up against the counter, I nibble on my scone and stare out the window, into the void of trees, waiting for the coffee maker to beep. Even though it's beautiful, there's an emptiness out here. Serene, but uninhabited. It's still beautiful to me. I've always loved living in the mountains and I don't think that will ever change. As I take in the rugged landscape, the coffee maker finally signals it's done brewing. Grabbing two coffee mugs, I fill one of them to the brim and leave the other one for Abs. No worries about running out of coffee; I made plenty for the both of us. I'm sure Abs will come down soon, since she turns into a bloodhound when there's coffee.

Blowing on it a bit to cool it off, I take a sip and about weep with gratitude. The first sip is like hot, black ambrosia. Grabbing the rest of my scone and my coffee, I plop myself into a chair at the dining table. Smoothing a hand over the surface, I murmur, 'Soon, you'll look all shiny and new.' The table might be old, but it has amazing details carved into it, along with carvings on the backs of the chairs. You can tell it was handmade. It just needs a little TLC.

Sipping my coffee, I disappear into my own mind, thinking about all the things I need to do. I don't have much time, but with Reese's help, I can make it happen. And that thought alone makes me positively giddy. I can't wait to start my new life. I've always wanted to own a B&B and now I finally do. I just have to get it going.

Spying a pad of paper and a pen, I start jotting down all the things I need to order and what else we need to do. And just when I've about exhausted my brain, I hear Abs shuffle down the stairs and across the great room, heading towards the kitchen.

She steps in, and I just have to laugh. She's borrowed a pair of my slippers and her hair is sticking up in all different directions. You'd think she had a wild night out, instead of a busy night in.

"Morning Sunshine," I say teasingly.

"Morning," she grunts, heading straight for the coffee. Grabbing the mug I sat out for her, she grabs the carafe and sloshes the black liquid into the mug, filling it just as full as mine. Aww, coffee. Nectar of the Gods.

Looking around, she spots my baked goodies and heads straight for them. Flipping open the lid, she takes out a blueberry scone and takes a huge bite, washing it down with coffee.

"Better?"

She sighs and turns around. "Much. Gonna need more coffee, though."

"Come sit," I say, motioning her to sit down. We need to come up with a game plan.

"Let's tackle the rest of the kitchen today. See if the appliances work. Then we can tackle the bathrooms. I'm thinking they're so old and gross, we should remodel each one. Almost new everything."

Her eyes go wide. "Can you afford all that?"

"I don't think I have much choice," I tell her. "The bathrooms are in pretty bad shape. With Reese helping, I can be open by the date I had in mind even with the bathroom renovations. People like vintage, not tired. And this place looks tired in a lot of areas. I don't want to be reviewed and called old and outdated. I want the place to be known as charming and rustic."

She nods.

"The kitchen needs remodeled, too, but it's still better than the bathrooms. "

She nods and gulps down more coffee.

She shrugs, patting her hair. "I need a shower."

"Me, too. I'll let you go first. Safe some hot water for me," I tease.

She smirks and gets up, taking her coffee with her.

With the time we had left during the weekend, we managed to get the fridge working and I also tested the range. The oven seemed to heat up okay, so we marked both of those items off the list. As with the bathrooms, I need to replace everything in the kitchen, as soon as I'm able to. But first, I need Reese to work his magic on the rest of the house. Then, he can work his magic on the kitchen, my favorite place of all.

Chapter 4

The doorbell chimes and I head to the front door, passing through the great room with its massive fireplace. Pulling on the heavy wooden door, I swing it open and Reese is standing on the front porch. He's wearing a flannel shirt over a t-shirt, soft/faded jeans, work boots, and his ever-present dimples.

"Good morning," I say, smiling as I swing open the screen door. "Come in."

"Thank you," he says, stepping inside.

"Let's head into the kitchen," I tell him. "We can sign all the paperwork there."

He follows me into the kitchen, pulling out a stack of papers and a pen.

"I'll just have you sign and date here," he points out, his finger showing me where to do so. "This is just giving me permission to work on the place. Once you show me what you wish to have done, I'll draw up another document, to show you what the initial estimate is. Then once we agree upon the number and projects, we'll both sign and date it. Then I can get started."

I nod. "There are quite a few things that need done around here."

"Let me guess...the bathrooms?"

"Yes, how did you guess!" I joke, shaking my head.

"Let's just say I had a hunch," he says, smiling.

I look into his eyes and they're twinkling. Do men's eyes twinkle? Reese's sure do.

"Great! Let me go through what we'd like to do."

"Sounds good," he says.

"First, we want to get all new floors, toilets, and vanities in each bathroom. Then, we'd like to pull up all the carpet and refinish the wood floors. Abs and I can paint. Then, we want to have the furniture that is usable sanded and painted, then reupholstered. Oh, and we also need to have you, or someone, check the hot water heaters and the furnace."

"Okay, that's doable."

"But wait, there's more."

"There always is," he replies, chuckling lightly.

"We also need to fix the paint on the outside of the house and repair the front porch railing and shutters. And after all that is said and done, the kitchen needs re-done."

He nods.

"Is that too much?"

"Not at all. I'll need to look around a bit more and price supplies. I can get you an estimate by the end of the week."

"But can you start today?" I ask, dismayed.

"I can. As long as you're okay with it."

"I am. You do good work. You come highly recommended."

"Then go ahead sign and date," he tells me, gently pushing the document toward me.

I reach for the pen at the same time he does and our fingers collide, a spark shooting between us. I jerk back, my eyes flying to his. Calmly, he picks the pen, laying it on top of the stack of papers for me to sign, his gaze never leaving mine. I can't seem to peel my eyes away, either. Reese has this look on his face that I've never seen before.

Shaking myself out my stupor, I pick up the pen, signing and dating the docs in front of me. Finished, I drop the pen back onto the counter. I don't know what to make of what just happened.

He nods. "Let me look around and take some notes. Then I'll check the hot water heater and the furnace."

"Thank you. Abs and I will be busy working on ripping up the carpet and working on painting. Let us know if you need anything. I'll leave the door unlocked, so you can come and go as needed."

He nods and takes off, heading upstairs. Shaking my head, I go in search of Abbie. I need to let her know I'm heading down the mountain, into town, to buy paint and supplies. I look around, but don't see her, so I text her.

Kelsie: I'm heading into town to get paint and supplies. Reese is here. You might stick around, to see if he has any questions.
Abbie: Can do. I'm just working on moving all the furniture to the garage.
Kelsie: Okay. I'm heading out.
Abbie: Bye [waving emoji]
Kelsie: [Smile emoji] [waving emoji]
Grabbing my jacket and purse, I head out the door.

As I drive down the mountain, I can't stop thinking about, well, pretty much everything. About the B&B. And especially about Reese. The other night at the bar, he looked so forlorn. But with what happened, I don't know what to think. He doesn't seem sad at all. I wonder made him so melancholy?

Pulling into a stall, I park my SUV and shut off the engine. Time to get down to business.

A bell tinkles as I open the door and as soon as I step inside, I'm greeted by Tim Smith, an older gentleman who's owned this very hardware store for years. It's been so long, I think he's owned it since before I was born. I can't say for sure, but it's been a good long time, I can say that much.

"Kelsie Marsh! I heard you were back in town. You bought the old Johnson place."

"Hi, Mr. Smith. You heard right. I want to restore it to its former glory as a B&B."

"Is that so?! Well, I'll be. That's great news! I hated to see the place sitting empty for so long."

"Me, too. It won't be sitting empty any longer."

He beams a smile at me. "And you need paint."

"Yes, sir. I'm keeping it simple with white. We'll add splashes of color with décor and fabrics."

"Well, then follow me. Let's get you everything you'll need."

"Lead the way," I say teasingly, gesturing for him to do so.

As I walk behind Mr. Smith, I can't help but smile. I can't wait to see the paint on the walls, shining fresh and clean. It's simple, but it'll make a world of difference.

"We'll start with this," he says, pulling out two five-gallon buckets of paint. "Will this be enough?"

I have to think about it for a moment. "Let's double it. I'm going to need painting supplies, too," I add.

He pulls down two more buckets and leaves them on the floor. "I've got these two," I tell him, picking them up. I follow him, my arms straining, to the front of the store.

"Just drop them here. Let's get you the supplies you'll need."

I follow him to the paint supplies. He scans the brushes, then picks out two of them.

"Two enough?"

"Let's do three," I tell him.

His eyebrows raise. "Someone else up there with you?"

I smile. "I've hired Reese Wilson."

"Have you now. He's a good one."

"Good to know," I say, shaking my head. "I'm also going to need painters tape, a ladder, and paint trays," I tell him.

He snags the items and carries them to the front. He rings me up and I have to hold back a sigh. *Do not think about money.* I hand him my card and he swipes it, then hands me my receipt.

"Let me help you out with this stuff," he tells me.

"Thank you, I appreciate it."

Grabbing everything, we haul it out and load it into the back of my SUV. Strapping on my seatbelt, I drive back up the mountain.

* * *

Back at the Reindeer Inn, I pull up beside Reese's truck and cut the engine. Getting out, I head inside to find Abs. She can help me unload.

"Abs, I'm back!" I don't hear anything back.

"Abs?" Still nothing. I wonder where she's at.

Walking back outside, I head to the backyard, where I spot her and Reese on the patio.

"Back again!"

Abs smiles. "Reese and I were just talking about what we should do with all this furniture. I think we can re-use some of it, while we just need to get rid of the others."

"I agree. Let's re-use these and these," I say, pointing to each one. "And get rid of the rest."

She nods.

"Reese?" I ask.

"I can refinish and reupholster them. No problem. You'll just need to let me know what color and what fabric you want to use."

I look at Abbie. "We can do that. And let's keep it simple. Let's paint them white. What do you think, Abs?"

"Simple is better. Besides, adding color with décor will work perfect, I think."

I chuckle lightly. "Great minds think alike."

"That they do."

As we chat, Reese watches us. Or me, rather. I truly don't know what to make of what happened between us earlier. Lost in thought, I see Abs shake her head at me.

"What?" I ask guiltily.

She laughs. "Never mind."

Reese clears his throat, hands on his hips. "You need help unloading?"

"Yes, actually. Abs and I can get it, though."

"Suit yourself."

I gesture to Abs. "Let's go."

Abs and I walk around the house, to where I'm parked in front of the garage.

"You could have let him help us," Abs tells me.

"I know. But he has better things to do."

"Maybe he wanted to help."

That stops me. "What makes you say that?"

"Oh, wow. Kels, I love you, but you are completely oblivious."

That gets my back up. "Oblivious to what, exactly?" I ask, my eyes narrowing.

"Reese," she whispers.

"What about him?" I whisper loudly back.

"He has a thing for you."

I guffaw. "For me? Yeah, right. We're old friends."

"No, really. You should have seen him when you walked around the side of the house. He heard you and he got the biggest smile on his face. I swear, the man can't stop smiling when you're around."

"Okaaay," I jest, laughing.

Lugging in all the paint and supplies, we sit them down near the front door.

"Where should we start?"

"Let's start in the bedrooms."

"And now we have to lug all this stuff upstairs. You should have taken up Reese's offer to help," she says, exhaling loudly. Clearly she's none too happy about it.

Abbie being *dramatic? Never!*

"We don't need all the paint, just one gallon to start. I can get the paint, if you can get the ladder. We can come back down for the supplies."

She doesn't reply, just grabs the ladder and heads up the stairs. Wisely, I grab the paint and let her be. I love my little sister, but she can be a little dramatic at times.

Getting all set up, we start painting and of course, Abs pulls a funny. Glancing over, I see a few bold strokes of the paint brush and then she steps back to admire her handiwork.

"What do you think?"

I step back and immediately start to laugh. "Wow, Abs. So subtle." She's drawn, with paint, a crude picture of a penis and balls. "I'm sure that'll go over well with guests," I say, laughing some more.

"Well," she says haughtily, faux-swinging her hair over her shoulder. "If you don't like my masterpiece..." she says, trying to keep a straight face.

"What was that?" I ask jokingly. "Did you say master-peen?" I reply, laughing so much, tears run down my cheeks.

"O.M.G.! Did you just call it..." she says, but can't finish.

We're both laughing so hard, we have to catch our breath. By the time we can breathe again, the paint has started to dry.

"I *sooo* did," I reply, drying my eyes. "We need to get moving or we'll never get this done. We have the entire rest of the house to do yet," I say, sighing. Abs sighs right along with me.

"Such a buzzkill!"

I shrug, going back to painting. We really do need to focus. But a few good laughs along the way is exactly what we both needed.

Chapter 5

The next day, Reese comes back and starts working on all the furniture, sanding and prepping them to be painted. All in all, six chairs, a large dining table, and eight dining chairs need to be refinished. And out of six chairs, all need reupholstered. Four out of the six will go back into each room and the remaining two chairs will be used in the great room in front of the fireplace. We got lucky that we can re-use quite a few pieces.

As Reese gets to work on the furniture, Abs and I get to work painting all the bedrooms in the house—from top to bottom. It takes the entire day to finish, but we manage. As I admire our handiwork, I can start to picture each room. One room will be blue and white, the next red and white, the next red and green and white, and the last red and black and white. Simple, yet classic.

* * *

The next day, the wind picks up and the sky looks heavy, like it wants to rain. It's early yet and Reese hasn't arrived. I hope he gets here soon, because the sky could open up at any moment. Living at this elevation, the storms can get nasty in a hurry. Late fall/early winter rainstorms aren't uncommon in these parts. And my point is made when all of the sudden, a streak of lightning flashes outside. Not two-seconds later, a giant boom rattles the windowpanes and ice-cold rain pelts the house. Rain is coming down in sheets and it's so heavy, I can barely see out the window. I'm glad Abbie stayed here last night, so she won't be caught unaware of the storm. Reese, however, could very well be driving up the mountain as we speak.

Lightning flashes and thunder crashes when I hear a loud knock on the door. I'm just glad I even heard it over the deafening booms outside.

Racing to the front door, my shoes slapping the wood, I grab the brass handle and swing open the front door.

"Oh, Reese," I gasp. He's drenched from the rain.

He doesn't reply, just walks inside and removes the door from my hand, shutting it.

Rubbing the water from his eyes, he says. "Morning."

"Um, good morning. You're just—"

"A tad soaked," he says, cutting me off. "You got a towel I could use?"

"Oh, yes. Be right back," I say, scurrying away to get him a towel, before the water dripping off him becomes a pond on the floor.

Grabbing two towels, I hurry back to the front door. As I turn the corner, I almost trip at the sight that greets me. Reese is standing there, shirtless, his muscles and smooth tan skin on display.

"I—"

He looks at me, reaching for one of the towels. I hand it off, my brain malfunctioning. I seem to have lost the ability to speak.

Thank goodness he speaks next. "Got a dryer? I need to dry my clothes."

"Um, yes I do."

He hands me his shirt and proceeds to unbutton his jeans, pushing them down. I just stand there stupefied, my cheeks heating up. Reese Wilson is stripping in my foyer! Getting my wits about me, I suddenly turn around, giving him my back.

"It's fine, Kels. It's not like you haven't seen it before," he says.

He's right. We used to strip down after our hikes and swim under the falls. It's a great memory. But last time I checked, Reese didn't look like he does now. He's not a boy. He's a grown man—with a grown man's body, muscles included.

"That's not the same," I mutter, my back still turned.

He gently turns me around, a hand on my shoulder.

"Hey. No big deal. We're both adults. I can put my wet clothes back on, if you want me to."

I look into his eyes. "Um, no. I can dry them for you. Do you want something to wear while they're drying?" I ask.

His eyebrows raise, then he smirks. "Um, Kels, I'm not exactly your size."

The awkwardness between us dissipates. "I know that. I have a hoodie you can wear. And probably a pair of sweats, too."

"And whose are they?" he asks, his voice lowering an octave.

"An ex. He wasn't as big as you, but they're better than nothing," I say, motioning with my hand. "Better than walking around in your boxer briefs," I tell him, eyeballing his crotch.

He shrugs. "Doesn't bother me. But if you've got them," he says nonchalantly.

"Coming right up," I tell him, sprinting to the stairs, taking them two at a time.

Opening up drawers, I pull out a pair of old sweats and a hoodie. I don't know if they'll even fit, since Reese is nothing like I remembered. He's no longer the tall and lean kid that I knew in high school. He's still tall, but now he's jacked, with a six-pack to die for.

Scooping up the clothes, I head back downstairs before Reese freezes to death. This old house is drafty on the best of days.

"Here you go," I say, handing him the sweats, and then the hoodie.

"Thanks," he says, smiling, his dimples peeking out.

Taking the sweats, he pulls them on. They're too short, but fit at the waist.

"Well, at least they fit," I quip.

"Sort-of," he grunts, pulling the hoodie over his impressive physique.

At least the hoodie fits him. For now, he's warm and dry. And I finally regain my ability to speak. Reese and his muscles are a dangerous distraction.

Reese

I checked the weather before I left and I thought I had enough time to drive up the mountain and get here before the skies unleashed. I was wrong.

I also thought I could make it to her front porch without getting too wet, but as I step onto her porch, I'm soaked, from head to toe. Wrong again.

So here we are, sitting in her kitchen, her pouring me a cup of coffee as I wear another man's clothes.

"Scone?" she politely asks me.

"Sure."

"And how do you like your coffee?"

"Black, thanks."

She bustles around the kitchen, the storm raging outside. It's a doozy of a storm. But it will pass soon, as these types of storms pop up suddenly and die out just as fast.

Kels hands me a cup of steaming coffee, then sets down a cranberry orange scone in front of me.

"Sorry about earlier. I didn't mean to make you feel uncomfortable," I tell her.

I really thought it was no big deal. Apparently, it was. Note to self: things are not the way they used to be.

She gives me a warm smile. "It's fine. I just wasn't expecting you to strip down in my foyer, that's all."

I cringe. When she puts it like that, it does sound bad.

"Again, I apologize. No more stripping in your foyer," I tell her.

She lightly laughs in response.

"And thanks again for the clothes."

"No problem. Your clothes should be dry soon."

I nod and take a sip of my coffee. Damn, that's some good bean juice.

"Your coffee is incredible. What kind is this?"

She beams. "It's actually a blend that was made especially for me. In Denver, I have a friend who roasts his own coffee beans and he roasted it just for me. He calls it the Reindeer Roast."

"Impressive."

Her grin gets even bigger. "And this place, the old Johnson place, will now be called the Reindeer Inn B&B."

I smile in return. "It has a nice ring to it."

"It does," she says proudly.

I take a few more sips of my coffee and finish my scone when Abbie walks in, doing a double take.

"What—"

"He got soaked by the storm. His clothes are in the dryer," Kelsie tells her.

I nod in affirmation.

She laughs and shakes her head, heading straight to the coffee pot.

I gulp down the rest of my coffee and stand. "Let me know when my clothes are dry," I say to Kelsie. "I'm going to get to work."

"Will do."

I leave Kelsie and Abbie and head to the garage. I need to finish prepping the furniture, then start painting every piece.

Kelsie

After Reese heads out to the garage to work on refinishing the furniture, Abs and I start painting the great room and foyer. In the middle of painting, I hear the dryer beep.

"I'll be right back," I tell her, going to get Reese's clothes out of the dryer.

Scooping them out, I make sure they're dry. And for some unknown reason, I bury my face in his soft Henley. As I do, I catch a hint of soap and masculine fragrance. The shirt still smells like him, even with getting soaked in the downpour. Sighing, I stop being a weirdo and bring Reese's clothes to him.

"How's it going?" I ask.

He looks up, happy to see me. "Good. Those my clothes?" he asks, reaching for a rag to clean off his hands.

"Yep. All dry," I say, waiting for him to clean off his hands, so that he can grab his clothes from me.

"Thank you, I'll go change. In the bathroom," he tells me, walking past me, into the house.

Well, that wasn't awkward or anything...

Heading back inside, I rejoin Abbie and get to painting. It takes us the rest of the morning and the afternoon to finish painting. After lunch, Abs and I rip up the old carpet.

"This is disgusting!" she says, waving her hand in front of her face, dispersing the dirty air. "This place is full of dust. Not to mention dust mites. Goodbye and good riddance!"

I cough. Dust is everywhere.

Stepping back out of the cloud of the dust, I reply, "It's a shame these gorgeous floors were covered. It really ties the place together. I'm just glad they can be refinished."

I can't wait for Reese to refinish the wood floors throughout the house. It will make all the difference.

She nods, coughing.

"Let's take a break. Let the dust settle."

"Good, because I need to pee," she says, laughing as she walks away.

I drop the carpet and padding and head to the kitchen for a drink of water. I'm parched. Propping a hip against the counter, I stare out the window as I drink my water. I really hope I can get this place up and running by January. By my approximation, I have about six weeks to get it going. I hope I haven't bit off more than I can chew. My water gone, I head back to ripping up carpet, ready to haul it away.

"Again, Kels. Reese could help us."

"Do we really need him to help? Besides, he went into town to order items for the bathroom. He's not here."

"Of course," she says, frustrated.

We're hauling out numerous rolls of old carpet and padding when Reese pulls up, parking out back. He must have bought a few supplies while he was there. We're on our last trip outside when Reese walks up behind me.

"Need help?" he asks us.

"No," I say.

"Yes," Abs says at the same time.

"Yes or no?" he says, looking back and forth between us.

I don't answer, struggling with the last and largest piece of carpet and padding. I grunt, trying to hold on, guiding it out the door. But when I'm about to get it through the door, the carpet starts to slip. I try to keep hold of it, but it's no use. It slips through my hands and off my shoulder, and as it does, the end of the carpet smacks Reese right in the face. He stumbles, but doesn't fall.

"Are you okay?" I ask, scared I've injured him.

His hand is covering his nose. Oh God, I've hurt him.

"I'm okay. Just a little blood. No big deal."

"Let me see," I say, gently pulling his hand away from his face.

He drops his hands and there's an angry red slash across his cheek and a bruise is forming under his eye. His nose is also bleeding.

He looks like he lost a fight. With a bear.

"I am so sorry. Come inside and let me clean you up."

I hold open the front door, ushering him inside. The carpet can wait. Leading him upstairs to my room, I beckon him inside.

"Have a seat on the bed. I have a first-aid kit," I tell him, disappearing into the bathroom.

I retrieve it and head back to Reese. "Again, I am so sorry. Does it hurt?"

"Not too bad. Just sore."

I nod, getting out peroxide and antibiotic ointment. "This may sting a little," I tell him, cleaning the scratches. He flinches a little bit when I dab at the deeper cuts, but otherwise just sits there.

"All done."

He nods, but doesn't smile. "I'd better get back to work."

I nod, heading back into the bathroom to put the first-aid kit away.

Once I'm back downstairs, I notice the old carpet is gone and so is Reese.

"Did Reese head out?" I ask Abs.

"Just back to the garage. Poor guy looks like he lost a fight with a bear. You really got him good, Kels."

"I know. I feel so bad!" I lament. "But I did clean up the scrapes."

"The least you could do," she tells me. "Now let's get cracking. We've got the hallways to paint."

I nod, soldiering on. I hope Reese isn't upset with me.

<h1 style="text-align:center">Chapter 6</h1>

By the end of the week, both Abs and I are tired and sore from all the cleaning and painting. But the place looks amazing. The new paint is simple, yet looks fresh and clean. Just the look I was going for. I can't wait to bring in the furniture. And speaking of Reese, he just got all the furniture refinished and re-upholstered. Talk about perfect timing. Now, we just need to haul them in and put them in each room. But Abs and I can do that tomorrow. It's Friday night and we deserve a much needed break.

After working all day, Abs and I clean up and get dressed and head into town. Sam's Place is the place to be on a Friday night in Foxtail Ridge. And I have to say, since I've moved back, the more I'm enjoying it. I'm seeing my hometown with fresh eyes. And I like what I see.

Settling into a booth, Abs and I order our beers.

"Food now or later?" I ask.

"Later. This beer is tasting extra good tonight," she says, taking a big gulp.

Good thing I drove tonight, because somebody is drinking a little too much, a little too fast. But I get it—it's been a week of back-breaking labor. And she's doing it for free. I don't blame her. She needs to blow off some steam. I'm cool with her doing that. As long as she doesn't get carried away.

As we drink our beer, I look around the bar, seeing all the locals. Wait, I'm a local, too. Even if I don't feel like it. But I am. It feels so foreign. As I'm looking around, I see Reese step inside and head to the bar. He's had a bit of a tough week, courtesy of my clumsiness. I still feel really bad about what happened.

I take a sip of my beer and the waiter stops by to ask if we'd like another round and Abbie answers before I even have the chance to say anything.

"Yes, please. Kels?" she asks, looking at me.

"Yes, please." I tell the waiter. "And two menus, also."

He nods and scurries off. The place is packed with people. I'm glad that Sam's Place stays pretty busy, even during times when the tourists aren't around. It's become a staple around here. Bored, Abs scrolls on her phone and I do the same, when a shadow falls over me. Looking up, I see it's Reese.

"Mind if I join you?"

I look into his deep blue eyes. "Sure," I say, scooting inward, making room on my side of the booth.

He sits down and scoots in, placing his beer on the table. "What are you ladies drinking tonight?" he asks, striking up a conversation.

"Locally brewed IPA," Abs answers.

"Locally brewed Stout," I tell Reese. "You?"

"Locally brewed German Hefeweizen."

"Cheers to local brewers!" I say, smiling and holding up my beer. Abs and Reese clink their pint glasses against mine and take a drink. "Cheers!"

After that, the waiter stops by and drops off our menus. He looks at Reese in question.

"I can use her menu," Reese tells him, gesturing toward me. "Give us a few minutes."

I peruse the menu and quickly decide on a steak, then hand the menu to Reese.

"Don't need it. I order the same thing every time I come here," he tells me, his eyes twinkling, his dimples on full display.

I shrug, laying the menu back down. Thank goodness it's dark in here, so the shiner I gave him is barely visible.

"How's the face?" I ask.

"Better. It's almost healed. Except for the black eye. But it's fading more and more each day."

"Again, I'm—"

"Don't apologize. It happened. It's no big deal. There have been other mishaps on job sites before. This is relatively minor."

I shut my mouth. I guess there's not much more to say. Good thing, too, because the waiter is back and ready to take our order.

"I'll have the spicy black bean burger with fries," Abs tells the waiter.

"And I'll have the KC strip. Medium-well."

"KC strip for me, also. Cooked medium."

"Anything else?" the waiter asks.

We all shake our heads no.

Reese

"So I meant to ask you sooner, but the week got away from me..." I say to Kels.

Abbie raises her eyebrows, curious what I'm about to ask.

Kels just studies me intently.

"There's a charity function on the first Saturday in December. Small business owners throughout the town come together to raise money for families in need. We do this at the annual Foxtail Ridge Christmas Festival. Since you're now a business owner, I thought we could team up for charity. How does that sound?"

Abs glances at us, then back down at her phone.

"What does all of this entail?" Kels asks me, genuinely interested.

"The town sells tickets to the Annual Christmas Festival and all items donated/sold during the festival raises money for underprivileged families."

"That sounds amazing!" Kels replies excitedly.

"I thought you'd like it." I say, giving her a smile.

"You've participated before?"

"I've never missed a year since I took over the family business."

"Count me in! Abs, you joining us?"

She shakes her head. "I'll be attending instead."

"Well, I guess it's just you and me then," Kels states.

"Works for me. I'll let Rosie, who's in charge, know that you'll be participating and that you can share my booth."

"Perfect. I can't wait!"

I nod happily. I can't wait to reveal my hobby; she has no idea what I do in my spare time. But I think she'll really like it.

Kelsie

Just as we're finishing up our conversation about the annual Foxtail Ridge Christmas Festival, Abbie's phone buzzes.

"Oh, hey. I'm sorry. I need to go. I'll just get my order to go."

"You sure?" I ask Abs.

"Yes. I need to talk with a new client on a potential project."

"Okay, then. Do you need a ride?"

"I guess I do. Can I have your keys? And Reese can take you home?"

I look to Reese in question.

"I can drive your sister home," he tells her.

"Great, thank you. I really need to get going," she tells us, sliding out of the booth. "I'll ask for my order at the bar."

She walks off, clutching her phone. I'm not sure what to say to Reese at the moment, so I ask more about the festival.

He tells me about last year's attendance and the record-setting amount they raised. I can't wait to be a part of it this year.

A few minutes later, the waiter drops off our steaks and we dig in. As we do, Reese makes polite conversation.

"So how was Denver. Miss it?"

"It was good. My job wasn't anything to write home about, but it paid the bills. I met a lot of new people while I worked there. Some I even called friends. Jody was one of those. There wasn't a Friday night we didn't go out and have a good time. But after a while, it just wasn't for me. I just wasn't into that scene anymore. And the city started getting so overcrowded with people, I couldn't even enjoy it anymore. Too many people, too much traffic. Too many rude attitudes. It was time to get out, so I jumped at the chance to move back here."

He nods. "The old Johnson place—" he says, but I politely interrupt him.

"You mean the Reindeer Inn," I say, smiling, giving him a wink.

"I stand corrected. The Reindeer Inn is a great opportunity to start over. I always wondered if someone would leap at the chance to open it again. Make it thrive. I'm glad to see you're that person," he says, smiling, showing off his dimples again.

Sigh. Reese and his dimples.

"How about you?" I ask.

"Not much to tell. Immediately after high school, I became emerged in the family business. I knew one day I'd take it over and I wanted to learn every little thing I could. Make it even better than it already was. I've branched out and it's grown. It's thriving, actually."

"That's amazing! I'm glad you found your place in this world. I hadn't really found mine until I landed on the old Johnson place. And the lightbulb just came on. I'd always loved that place when I was a kid. And now it's mine. Some days, I feel like it's a dream. I can't wait to open my doors!" I tell him, excitement lacing my voice.

"That's great, Kels. I'm glad you're back," he tells me.

"Me, too."

He lifts his pint to his lips, but my next question stops him, his pint glass suspended in mid-air.

"And what about a lady in your life? I hear you're single. I find that hard to believe. The great Reese Wilson. Single. What happened? I figured you'd be married with at least one kid by now."

I see him visibly tense. "I could say the same about you," he says, lifting the pint glass to his lips, taking a healthy gulp of his beer.

"Touché," I say, taking a healthy gulp of my own beer.

"I find that hard to believe. The ladies around here, they practically throw themselves at you. Not even a nibble?" I tease.

He shrugs. "No one ever caught my eye," he says, cutting into his steak, all but closing the door on the conversation.

I get asked the same thing all the time, too. Single and no kids. Like something is wrong with me. Newsflash, I just haven't met the right one yet. And I'm not going to settle. It's not in my nature.

I shrug back. I guess we both don't want to talk about it. So I do the next best thing—I ask about his family.

"How's your sister?" I ask, changing the subject.

"She's good. Married to a guy she met in college. They have two adorable kids—one boy and one girl. I'm Uncle Reese now," he says, his smile reaching his eyes. I can tell his family, his niece and nephew especially, make him happy.

"That's wonderful. I always liked your sister. She was such a sweetheart."

"Still is," he tells me.

Reese and I chat a few more minutes, then finish off our beers. As we do, the waiter drops off the check.

"Allow me," he tells me, grabbing the check.

"Reese, no," I plead.

"It's done," he tells me, placing his card in the tray.

"Well, thank you," I tell him. "Next time, dinner's on me."

Reese

Next time. Those two words are exactly what I wanted to hear. Maybe there's hope yet. Now, I just need to convince Kelsie she's the woman for me. But that's easier said than done.

On the drive back to the B&B, I see Kels getting drowsy. I know she's been busting her ass to get the old place in shape. She's tired, so I focus on the road and let the gentle hum of the road lull her to sleep. We've barely gotten halfway up the mountain, when I hear a little snuffle. Looking over, I see her head lulled to one side, her eyes closed, her mouth slightly open. She's not snoring, but she is breathing a bit heavy, making a slight snuffling sound. And it's adorable. I take another peek, then let her rest.

Kelsie

"Kels, time to go inside," Reese murmurs near my ear.

My eyes flutter open and I'm momentarily disoriented. Oh, that's right. I'm in Reese's giant work truck and he drove me home.

"Okay," I murmur back, reaching for my seatbelt. "Sorry. I didn't mean to fall asleep," I say, yawning.

"It's okay. Here, let me help you," he tells me, unbuckling my seatbelt and gently lifting me out of his truck and into his arms.

"I can walk," I say softly.

He ignores me and carries me to the front door. Magically, he has my keys and unlocks the door, heading inside. Kicking the door shut with his foot, he climbs the steps, each creaking under our combined weight.

Striding down the hall, he walks us into my bedroom and deposits me on the bed.

"I'm good Reese. Thanks for the ride home," I tell him sleepily, getting drowsy again, barely able to stay sitting upright. I'm not drunk, just tired. It must have been the beer. It's the ultimate sleep aid.

"You're welcome. Are you sure you want to stay here all alone tonight?"

I shrug. It's no different than all the previous nights. But I don't tell him no.

"That settles it then," he tells me, helping me out of my jacket, as I push off my shoes. Quicker than I can blink, he swings my legs under the covers and tucks me in.

"I'm staying. Do you have another bed?" he asks me.

I shake my head no.

"Scoot over," he tells me, discarding his jacket and shoes. But he doesn't stop there. He also shucks his jeans, then pulls off his shirt, leaving him in his boxer briefs.

Maybe if I wasn't so tired...

I scoot over and he slides into the bed beside me, gently moving me into his arms. I sigh, snuggling my butt against his front. He's so warm, he's like a furnace.

And that's the last thing I remember before sleep overtakes me.

Reese

Kels falls asleep almost instantly, and I'm left with her tight little buns pressed against my crotch. It's the sweetest kind of torture. But to have her in my life again is the greatest gift. Now, I just have to convince her to be mine. With that thought, I drift off to sleep, a smile on my face.

Chapter 7

THE NEXT MORNING

KELSIE

I wake up and I'm cocooned in warmth. I savor the feeling, then my eyelids pop open. What the...then it hits me. Reese stayed with me last night. Slowly shifting, trying to not wake him, I turn and gaze at his sleeping form. He looks so peaceful when he sleeps. As I'm admiring him, my mind drifts back to when we were younger, when we went sledding, even though we were way past the age to be doing so.

"Come on, Kels. You're never too old to go sledding!" Reese teases me.

"But—"

"No buts. Let's go!" he tells me, grabbing my gloved hand in his, the old timey metal and wooden sled in his other hand.

Leading me up the mountain, I follow him as he makes

tracks through the freshly fallen snow. It's fresh powder so the place isn't open to skiers.

Stamping up the mountain, I follow him, my hand still in his. Just when I'm about to throw in the towel, he stops and turns. "Here. Right here is perfect," he tells me, a huge smile on his face, his dimples showing.

"Reese, this is dangerous. It just snowed last night. There could be an avalanche at any moment. That's why the sign was there," I tell him, worried.

"Don't worry, Kels. This is going to be epic!" he tells me excitedly. "Just once. I won't drag you up here again."

I nod. Just this once.

Dropping the sled onto the snow, he climbs on then scoots back, making room for me in front of him. "Hop on," he tells me, patting the wooden slats in front of him.

I climb on, my legs tucked against my chest, and my feet against wooden the rungs in front of me. I feel him move forward, reaching in front of me to grab the rope. As he loops his arms around me, his front presses against my back. He's so close, I can feel his warmth through his jacket, even though it's freezing out here.

"Ready?" he asks, the warmth of his breath on my ear causing me to shiver.

"Ready," I breathe, my breath a white plume in front of me.

I feel him dig his boots into the snow and push off and soon, we're soaring down the mountain, gliding so fast, the landscape is zooming by. Even though I'm wearing a hat, my hair still flies outward from the sheer speed we're moving. I smile and hold on tight. Even though I'm nervous, I trust Reese to keep me safe.

And he does. As we near the bottom he plants his feet, slowing us down. We lose momentum, the sled coming to a halt, but not before it tips sideways, causing us to fall over into

*the powdery snow. We both laugh. As I struggle to sit up, he
tugs me back down, into his arms.*

"Admit it. That was fun!" he teases me.

*I knew it'd be fun. I just wasn't sure about how safe it was
going to be. But nothing happened, so we're okay.*

*"Yes, it was fun. Now let me up," I tell him, pulling out of
his arms.*

He lets go, helping me up.

I hadn't thought about our sledding excursion in years. But
now that I have, it brings a smile to my face.

"What's put that beautiful smile on your face this morning?" Reese asks me, his voice deep and rumbly.

"I was just thinking about us. When we were younger."

"Which part?"

"The time you took me sledding on that old metal sled
with wooden slats. That thing hauled!"

"I remember that day. And yes, my granddaddy's sled sure
did haul ass," he replies. "Love that thing."

"You still have it, don't you? The sled."

His whole face lights up. "Sure do. Now I take my niece
and nephew on it. Of course, we don't go near as far, or as
fast."

"OMG, Reese!" I squeal. "Say you'll take me sledding
again!"

"Of course I will!"

"Thank you, Reese."

He gives me one his potent smiles that about melts my
ovaries. *Wow!*

"You got some of that delicious coffee?" he asks, stretching, the blanket sliding down dangerously.

And of course he doesn't bother with the blanket; he just

lets the blanket fall away, revealing his glorious self, clad only in boxer-briefs. Embarrassed to be caught staring, I look away and get out of bed. Peeking at him under my lashes, I see him smile and scratch his abs. He's such a man's man.

Reese

I stretch, ready for some coffee. Throwing back the covers, I suddenly remember that I'm only in my boxer briefs and it's cold as ice in here. Bending down, I snag my jeans and shirt, then head downstairs. While Kels is in the bathroom, I'll get the coffee started.

As I stand in the kitchen, the coffee maker gurgling, I hear a key in the front door. And no sooner does it register, Abbie pops her head into the kitchen.

"Oh hey, Reese. You're here early," she says, studying me. She can tell I'm still in the same clothes as yesterday. This must be what women call the walk of shame.

"Your sister is upstairs," I tell her, going back to watching the coffee maker brew. Maybe if I ignore her, she'll go away. It's not like anything happened last night.

"You know, I can tell you stayed here last night," she says, surveying me.

"I did. Didn't want your sister staying here all alone last night."

"Sure, Reese. That's why you stayed."

I shrug, my back still turned. God, this is awkward. Nothing even happened. But she doesn't know that. It's none of her business, anyway.

Taking a hint, she heads out. Finally gone, I pour myself a cup of coffee and grab a bite to eat. I wanted to serve Kels breakfast in bed, but Abs interrupted us.

• • •

Kelsie

I open the door and expect to see Reese, but instead my sister is sitting on the bed, eyeing Reese's boots on my bedroom floor.

"Spill it!" she demands.

"Nothing to spill. Nothing happened. I fell asleep and he stayed the night. That's it."

"Seriously?"

"Seriously, Abs. he was just being a good friend. He brought me home after you bailed last night."

She gets a wicked grin on her face.

"You—"

"I did," she smirks. "But you didn't seal the deal."

"Dammit, Abs. I don't need you playing matchmaker."

"You sure about that? Next time, seal the deal Sis! He's a sure bet. He's been checking you out ever since you came back to Foxtail Ridge!"

I blush. Reese really does have feelings for me; I was just too blind to see them. This changes everything.

<h1 style="text-align:center">Chapter 8</h1>

Abbie and I join Reese in the kitchen for breakfast. It's a little awkward, but we manage. Over scones and coffee, we come up with a plan to finish the rest of the bed and breakfast in two weeks' time, so that I can have an open house before Christmas and then be fully open in January.

That afternoon, Reese works on finishing up the furniture and then moves on to the bathroom remodels. While he's busy with that, I order everything I'm going to need for the B&B: towels, toiletries, paper goods, and anything else that I think my guests will need. I also order a brand new, industrial-sized espresso machine that I think will be a big hit with my coffee drinking guests. Of course, I also order plenty of tea-both caffeinated and decaffeinated. I also order mattresses. I want my guests to feel welcome and comfortable.

Tomorrow, Abbie and I plan to drive to Denver to go shopping for the B&B. And I can't wait! It's going to be so much fun to decorate this old place. While we're gone, Reese is also going to refinish the floors. Then once we come back, we can start getting all four bedrooms set up. Even though the bathrooms aren't done, Reese can still work on them at the same time as Abs and I start to make this place cozy and comfortable.

DENVER

Pulling into a parking stall, my heart rate speeds up. I'm excited to finally be able to decorate, but my poor credit card is going to take a beating. It'll be worth it, though.

"Ready?" Abs asks, clearly seeing that I'm about to have a panic attack.

"Kels, Are you sure about this? We can always buy half of what you mentioned. You can always add stuff later," she tells me, reassuringly.

I take deep breath. Everything is going to be fine. I can do this.

"Let's go," I tell her, getting out of the SUV.
Don't think about the cost. It'll all be worth it.

"One for me and one for you," Abs, says, pulling out two carts. "Where do you want to start?"

"Let's start with lighting. Then do pillows, blankets, stuff like that. Then look for other types of décor."

She nods. "I'll take the black, white, and red room. And the red and green room. You can have the other two: the green and white room, and the blue and white room."

She smiles, bulldozing her way right through. That's Abs for you.

"Sure. And every room will soon have names, so it won't be so hard to remember which room is which," I tell her.

"Do tell. Are you naming them after Christmas carols? Or old-timey holiday movie references? You're killing me with the suspense, here! Put a girl out of her misery, will ya?!"

Abs is all fired up.

"Fine," I say, rolling my eyes, letting out a little laugh. "The rooms will be named after some of Santa's Reindeer: Dasher, Vixen, Cupid, and of course, Rudolph."

"The guests are going to love that! Let's *do* this!" she exclaims excitedly, rubbing her palms together.

She grabs ahold of her cart and pushes off, power walking through the store, making a beeline for the holiday section. Not to be left behind, I grab my cart and follow. This is going to be fun. Hard on my pocketbook, but fun, nonetheless.

Abbie slows down and stops. "I'm going to start here. I'll let you handle the lamps."

I nod and head toward the section where lamps line the shelves, lit up and shining like a beacon. Slowly walking through, I see many different styles, colors, and themes. Not sure about what I want for the other rooms, I do know I want silver metal for the blue and white room. And black metal for the black and red room. And the other two, I think, will have a bronze, rustic look to them. Maybe wood and metal or just wood. All a little different, but all very much tied into each theme. Browsing a little more, I snag four lamps, one for each room.

That done, I head toward the pillows and blankets. Rolling into the aisle, I notice a comforter set right away. It's soft and fluffy, with black and white buffalo plaid. Grabbing it off the shelf, I pull it forward and notice another one behind it, but in red and white. Perfect! I maneuver both into my cart, then spy more colors further down the aisle. Another one is grey and white buffalo plaid. That one will work in the blue room. Now, I need find one last set. I look and don't see any other colors in buffalo plaid. However, I do spy a green and red traditional plaid one. It will work. That done, I pick out multiple sets of sheets and wedge them into my already full cart, along with pillows.

Spinning my cart around, I go in search of Abbie. Spotting her, I roll up to a stop. "Wow, Kels, those will work great!" she says, looking over the items. "We should get you another cart."

"I think I'm going to just check out, take the stuff to my SUV, then come back in."

"That works, too," she says to me, her back turned. She's intent on finding more décor.

Heading to the front of the store, I join the line to check out. When it's my turn, I pull out each item and lay them on the counter. The cashier wrestles with them, then hands them back to me, since there is limited space on the checkout counter. She scans the last item, then rattles off the total. My eyes about bulge when I hear her. But it's not any higher than I thought it would be. Pulling out my credit card, I insert it into the machine, paying for everything.

Back inside the store, I find Abbie still in the holiday section, so I head back to the pillows and blankets. I'm not sure what I want to include, so I browse the blankets. I decide on white, fluffy faux fur blankets. Grabbing four of them, I toss them into my cart, then go in search of Abs.

"Finding anything good?" I ask. I know she's found stuff, judging by the insane amount of stuff in her cart.

"Oh, Kels. Yes. Check this out!" she says excitedly.

Digging into her cart, she pulls out a rustic looking sign and holds it up proudly. It has a reindeer on it with pines in the background. Above the reindeer, it says *Reindeer Inn*. And below the reindeer, it says *Bed & Breakfast*.

"OMG, Abs! That's perfect! I love it!" I exclaim so loud, it comes out more like a squeal. I can't help it, I'm excited. So excited, I grab it out of her hands and put it into my cart.

"Hey now, easy with that thing," Abs teases.

I laugh. "Can't let that one out of my site. Oh, and what do you think about these?" I say, stroking the soft fabric of the throw blankets.

"I like 'em. Oh, they're *sooo* soft!" she says, grinning, stroking the soft fabric. "These could be used—"

"Don't even say it," I say, cutting her off. "I don't want to know what guests will be doing in each room. Gross, Abs!"

"Gotta scratch that itch sometime!" Abs says, laughing, looking at me pointedly.

I shrug my shoulders. I really don't want to know. Changing topics, I ask Abs what else she's found.

"Found these holiday wreaths. One for each door."

"Good idea. Anything else?"

"I sure did!" she says excitedly, digging around in her cart. "I also found these cute throw pillows and matching stockings for each room. What do you think?" she gushes, holding up 4 sets of stockings, one set for each room.

"I love them!" I tell her. And I do. Each set coordinates with each room and are woven with holiday and winter designs. Reindeer, snowflakes, Christmas trees, gingerbread men, and ornaments to name a few. They're adorable!

"I haven't found much else, except for a few little shadow boxes with cute sayings. But I was thinking we could make a large framed picture of each room's name. For above the bed."

"Yes! And maybe we could make one for each door. So guests know which room they'll be staying in."

"Exactly!" she says, holding up her hand for a high-five.

Ever the dutiful sister, I don't leave her hanging. I hold up my hand and lightly smack my palm to hers in solidarity. Taking a few seconds, I go over my mental checklist. Have I forgotten anything? *Yes, yes I have.*

"I totally forgot to buy rugs for each room and bathroom. Let's get those, too."

Finally shopped out, at least at this store, I say, "Let's head to the front and pay, then move on to the next store. I want to buy a small Christmas tree and decorations for each room."

She nods, pushing her cart ahead of me toward the front of the store. We check out and my credit card groans under the pressure. *Again.* Piling everything into my SUV, we head to the next store.

Pushing our carts through the next store, we find the aisle with the faux Christmas trees and get to shopping. I would love to have real, live trees in each room but I know some people are allergic, so plastic trees it is. But I am definitely putting a real one in the foyer. Looking up and down the aisle I spot smaller ones, about four feet tall. They'll fit perfectly in the corner of each room. I pick up four of them and drop them into my cart. Next, we shop the ornament aisle. Overwhelmed, I make a quick decision.

"You know what? I say we keep it simple. And classic."

Abs looks and me and just shrugs. She doesn't really care either way.

"We can add more to it, later."

She nods, bending down to snag a box of glass ornaments.

"Like this?" she asks, holding up red and green ones.

"Yes. But also blue and silver. And white."

Gently laying the box in the cart, she snags additional boxes for each tree, keeping with the colors for each room.

"And for the rest, let's grab reindeer and Santa ornaments. And snowflakes. And sleds. Let's keep it winter and Christmas themed," I tell her.

"Do they all have to be the same?"

"No. They can be all different kinds, sizes, and colors. As long as they're not ugly, it's fine with me."

She gives me a jaunty salute and wades through the glut of ornaments, while I look for lights. Loaded down, we have everything we need to decorate four mini Christmas trees and a standard sized tree. Ribbon, lights, and ornaments included. In the end, we've got everything we need. And then some.

"What's next?" Abs asks.

"Let's get decorations for the tables. I'm thinking candles, lanterns, and wreathes."

She nods, heading toward the kitchen section. Browsing, we find enough decorations for the tables. And so finally, after almost five hours, we're done shopping.

With Abbie's help, I lug the rest of our purchases outside and load them into my SUV. It's pretty much filled to the brim, which is almost comical because I still haven't gotten everything I need for the B&B—I still need tableware for my guests. It seems I have more shopping to do. But since I need items in bulk, I'm going to just order the rest. Tired, yet happy, it's time to head home. Back to Foxtail Ridge.

Chapter 9

FOXTAIL RIDGE

REINDEER INN

When we get back, Reese is still there, even though it's way past five o'clock. I don't hear anything, but that doesn't mean Reese isn't hard at work. By now, he's probably gotten a good portion of the floors sanded. Heck, he might even be refinishing the floors already.

Walking in the front door, I see Reese applying stain to the newly sanded floor. And what he's done already looks amazing! The place is really starting to come together!

"Hey, Reese. Looks good!" I tell him.

He looks up at me. "It's turning out beautifully."

"It is," I say, smiling. My heart is so full at the moment, I can't say much else.

"Did you find what you were looking for?" Reese asks me.

"We did. Not quite everything, but we can order the rest."

"So how far have you gotten?" I ask.

"I finished the upstairs. Now, I've only got the first floor to finish. I should be able to finish this tonight."

I nod. "And how long does it take to dry?"

"About that. You'll need to stay off the floors until tomorrow."

"So I can't stay here."

"Afraid not."

"I'm sure I can stay with Abbie tonight. Right Abs?" I say, turning my eyes to her.

"Um, I have to meet with an international client. Time zone differences. I don't want to keep you up tonight."

"You can stay with me," Reese offers.

I can feel Abbie's eyes on me.

"I don't want to put you out."

"You won't be. You can just ride into town with me once I'm done."

"Sounds good to me, Kels," Abs says, backing toward the door. "I'm going to head home, get a bite to eat. Do a little work. I'll see both of you tomorrow," she says, ducking out of the door.

Reese looks at me. "Okay with staying with me?" he asks.

"You're sure you don't mind?" I say tiredly, not sure this a good idea.

"Absolutely."

"If you say so..."

"I do. Let me finish up here and we can go."

I nod. "I'll just pull my SUV into the garage."

He smiles and goes back to working on the floors.

Reese

I finish up the floors and start to clean up. As I wipe my hands with a rag, I hear Kelsie walk into the doorway and stop. I don't turn around, just continue to clean up. I know she's watching me; I can feel her eyes on me, practically burning a hole through me. It doesn't bother me in the slightest. She can look all she wants. And she can have me, if she wants me. All I ever wanted was her. My feelings haven't changed since we were in high school.

"Ready to go?" I ask, turning around. For good measure, I give her one of my signature smiles, but with a little added smirk, just for her. Of course, my dimples are probably showing, which I know she secretly loves.

"Yep. And you're sure you don't mind?"

"Not even a little bit," I tell her, tucking the rag away. I've been wanting to bring Kelsie by my place since she got back, but there hasn't been the right opportunity to do so. But now the timing is right.

"I'm done here, let's go," I say, walking toward her, taking her in from head to toe. She's still standing framed in the doorway, leaning against the door jamb, her arms crossed. She's relaxed and a bit tired around the edges, I can tell, but that doesn't stop me from enjoying the view. With her arms crossed, it pushes her breasts upward, where the tops peek out from the v of her shirt. I don't linger long, but the image of her leaning against the door jamb is seared into my mind. It's an image I'll be adding to my collection, just like the rest of my memories of her.

She pushes away from the door jamb and walks out, and I follow her, close on her heels. As she's about to hoist herself into the cab, I gently grasp her waist and hoist her into my truck.

"Reese, seriously. I can get into your truck just fine," she tells me, giving me a scolding. She even throws in *that* look. I ignore her.

"I know," I reply, walking to the driver's side door. It's getting harder and harder to keep my hands off her sweet curves. I've wanted her for so long, it's damn tough not touching her.

As I drive down the mountain, I use the time to catch up.

"How was your day? Find stuff for the B&B?"

"Did we ever! My poor credit card is crying uncle right now," she tells me, laughing softly.

"I'll bet. Everything is Christmas themed, right? You picked the perfect time of year to open. The stores are brimming with holiday stuff right now."

"I know! It *is* perfect!"

"Have you had dinner?"

She looks at me. "No, actually," she replies. And at that moment, her tummy rumbles. *Loudly*.

"I haven't either. How about I make us some dinner at my place. A little food and beverage and a little rest. How does that sound?"

She looks over at me and gives me a grateful smile. "That sounds amazing. Are you sure it's not too much trouble? I'm already begging a room from you for the night. And now dinner."

"That's what friends are for, right?!" And as soon as it comes out of my mouth, I want to kick myself. I don't want to be just friends. I want to be hers. As in forever.

"I suppose so," she says wistfully.

The rest of the drive is quiet so I turn on the radio, keeping the volume low. Kelsie seems okay with it, so I let her be. I know she's had a long day. I give her a quick glance and focus on getting us safely down the mountain.

Pulling into my driveway, I come to a stop and place my truck in park, shutting it off. Glancing over at Kels, I see her face light up with happiness.

"Oh, Reese! You live in an A-frame!"

I smile. "Yes, I do."

I really do love my little place. It's not huge, but it's modern and cozy. And my nearest neighbors are over a mile away, so there's that, too.

"That is so cool!" she exclaims, unbuckling her seatbelt and slinging open her door.

I get out the same time she does, but she's too quick for me. I would have loved the chance to help her out of my truck. I don't mind, though, because she'll be in my arms later tonight.

Unlocking the door, I swing it open wide and gesture her inside. If she thinks the outside is something, wait until she sees the inside. I worked with an interior designer to complete the inside.

I hear Kels gasp and turn around sharply. "Reese! It's gorgeous! I love all the modern furnishings!"

"Thank you. I thought you might like it," I say, blushing slightly. That's the power Kels has over me. I, a grown man, blushing. Only for her.

"I absolutely do! Did you do all the interior design yourself?"

I let out a low chuckle. "I wish, but no. I had some help."

She looks at me intently. "May I ask who it was? I'd love to pick their brain."

"A friend of mine, his sister, is an interior designer, did all of it." I conveniently leave out the part where she tried to get me to go out on a date with her. I let her down gently, but apparently not gently enough since I haven't heard from her since. But hey, it's not my fault women fall at my feet. My heart belongs to only one woman—the one currently standing in front of me. I just hope she feels the same way.

"Well, she did a fantastic job!"

I nod, agreeing. She really did.

"Let me change clothes and I'll be back in a few to make

dinner. Have any preferences?" I ask, walking up the stairs, to the loft, where my bedroom is. My home is an open concept design, so I'll still be able to hear her from up here.

I don't immediately hear a response, so I know she's thinking. Striding to the back of the loft, I strip my shirt over my head and unsnap my jeans, when I hear her voice float through the air, toward my loft.

"What are my choices?" she asks, a playfulness to her voice.

Shirtless, I walk over to the loft railing, and peer down at her.

"Steak, chicken, pasta. You name it, I've probably got it."

She peers up at me, zeroing in on my bare chest and torso.

I run my hand over my pecs and abs, giving her a little tease. And her eyes track my every movement. Oh, Kels. You're too easy.

"How about I grill some steaks. And I think I've got a salad for a side. If that works for you."

She blinks, snapping out of her trance. "Um, yes. I think that'll work just fine," she replies, licking her lips.

Oh, so we're a little thirsty, hmm? Thirsty for me, I hope.

"I can do that. Have a seat if you want. If you're thirsty, you're welcome to raid my fridge."

She doesn't answer, just walks off. I hope she's as hot for me as I am for her. Because the last few years have been downright torturous for me.

Pulling off my dirty jeans, I replace them with a clean pair and pull on a fresh shirt, tugging it over my head. That done, I head downstairs to start cooking.

When I enter my kitchen, I love the scene before me. Kels, a drink in her hand, is sitting on one of my barstools. She looks relaxed.

"What you got there?" I ask, curious if she popped open the wine that my sister left in the fridge the other night.

"Some kind of wine that was in your fridge. Probably left by some chick," she says, taking a sip of said wine.

I raise my eyebrows at her. "I'll have you know it was not, in fact, some random chick. My sister left it in there a couple of nights ago. I don't bring random chicks here," I tell her, emphasizing "random chicks" with air quotes.

"So what do you do then? Get a hotel room for the night? Love 'em and leave 'em?"

Okay, now she's starting to piss me off. "Okay, Kels. Enough. I don't do random hook-ups."

"Then what do you do?"

I deflect instead. "And what about you, Miss I moved to Denver and left everyone behind?"

She laughs. "I dated a few guys. No one caught my interest."

I give her a pointed look. She finally drops it.

"I'm going to start dinner," I tell her, leaving our little impromptu convo behind. "You're welcome to sit there or out in the great room."

Walking into the great room, I follow Kels and get a fire started, stoking it until it roars with warmth, flames licking upward. Wood crackles and the faint scent of wood smoke floats through the air.

"I'm going to start the grill."

Kels just bobs her head and takes another sip of her wine.

I head outside to my patio out back and fire up the grill. As it's getting hot, I grab the steaks and the lettuce. After prepping the steaks, I grab the lettuce and chop some veggies for the salad. Glancing outside, I see the grill isn't hot enough yet, so I set about making the salad. As I'm doing so, I peer toward Kelsie, to see what she's up to. Not much, from the look of it. But that's okay, since I want her to relax. She's been working her ass off and deserves a night of rest and relaxation.

I glance outside and the grill is almost hot enough, but not quite. Pulling out tableware, I set the table. When she hears me sit the plates down, her head snaps toward me.

"I'm a terrible guest. Let me help."

"Thank you, but that's not necessary. Besides, everything is pretty much done," I reply, walking back into the kitchen. It's time to get our steaks on the grill.

Walking back outside, I open the grill and slap the steaks onto the grates, eliciting a sizzle from each one. The steaks should be done in less than 10 minutes. Closing the lid, I walk back inside. And Kelsie is there, bending over, peering into my fridge. Her ass looks delectable. I have to stop myself from cupping the sweet globes. It's one of the hardest things I've had to do as of late.

"Something I can help you find?" I ask, startling her.

She pops up, stepping back from the fridge. "I was looking for the salad dressing."

"Right here," I reply, reaching toward the shelves that line the door. Inadvertently, my arm brushes her breast and we both freeze.

Her eyes dart to mine. I grab the salad dressing and step back. I'm not sure what to say. But I know she felt the same spark of sexual awareness that I did. There's definitely something between us. There's no denying it.

I hand her the bottle and turn to reach for a glass in the cabinet to the right of the sink. I need to cool down, since the temp in here has suddenly risen a few degrees. It has nothing to do with the fire roaring in the great room and everything to do with Kels and me. What's brewing between us.

I pour myself some water from the fridge and take a big gulp. The longer I'm around Kels, the more I want her. And with what just happened, I think she wants me, too. She wouldn't have asked about the chick who brought the wine if she didn't care. If people don't care, they don't make a big deal about something. But she did bring it up and that was her way of asking about my sexual history. Newsflash: there isn't much to tell. I'm not a monk, but I don't do random hookups.

I check the time on my phone; it's time to flip the steaks. Sitting my glass down on the counter, I grab a plate and tongs, heading back outside. In no time at all, the steaks are done. Once I'm back inside, I let the steaks rest for a few minutes. Might as well grab a beer. And maybe Kels needs more wine.

"More wine, Kels?"

"Sure," she answers, getting up off the couch. "Dinner ready?"

"Yep. Help carry things to the table?" I ask her. I really don't need help. But I don't want her to feel bad for not helping.

I fill her wine glass, then grab the steaks and my beer. She grabs the salad and the dressing.

Sitting down, we both dig in. Not much is said, but there's really not much to say. I drink my beer and she sips her wine as we eat. Pretty normal stuff. But I'm enjoying it immensely. Not the eating part, but spending the time with Kels part. I've missed her.

"Great steak," she tells me, sitting back.

I give her a smile. "Glad you liked it."

"Now I'm getting sleepy."

"You're welcome to get cozy on the couch. I can clean up."

"I will. Right after I help clean up. You cooked, so I should clean up."

"Up to you."

She answers by pushing her chair back and grabbing my plate and hers. I follow her with our glasses and the salad dressing. We load everything into the dishwasher and put away the rest of the salad. It takes less than five minutes.

"There," she says. "Now we can both relax."

I give her a grateful smile and gently take her hips, scooting her toward the edge of the kitchen. She takes the hint and walks into the great room, hips swaying. And I watch her with every step she takes. I can't peel my eyes away.

She plops down on my couch and I join her on the other end, even though I'd rather her be in my arms. But there'll be time for that very, very soon.

I haven't finished my beer yet, so I take a swig from the bottle and look at her. She has her wine with her, but she doesn't take a sip, just looking at me like she wants to say something, but doesn't know how. I feel you, Kels. I'm the same way. There's so much I want to say, but I'm not sure how.

Luckily for me, she breaks the silence. "So how about our classmates. How many are still around? I've been so busy with the B&B I haven't had much of a chance to find out."

I settle in, sitting back. "Quite a few actually. Remember Whitney? She married Travis. And Blake? He married Christy. And Jake? He's not married, but he's still around. Big shocker on both accounts, I'm sure. There's a few more, but I'm not sure what they're up to. And now you're back here, too."

"Blake and Christy. Didn't see that one coming. They're like oil and water. Maybe that's what makes them work."

"Maybe," I reply, taking another gulp of my beer. "So what about you. Why the sudden urge to move back here from Denver?"

"I just got tired of city life. I loved the frenetic pace, but I was ready to slow down. And I knew Foxtail Ridge was the place to come back to. It's home."

"Got your kicks, now you're back. For good."

"Pretty much."

"Well, I'm glad you're back."

"Me—" she says, starting to yawn. She yawns so big, her cute little jaw cracks. "Oh, my. Excuse me. It must be the day and the wine. It *does* feel good to be back."

"And what about you. I know why you stayed, but you're single. Never married? You never got married, right?"

"Nope. Never married. Single as can be."

"Same. Single as can be. Who knew we'd be thirty-somethings, never married and no kids!"

I don't answer, because it was never my intent. But I just couldn't be with anyone who wasn't Kelsie.

I smile and finish my beer. "Hey, I'm going to head out to my workshop. You're welcome to make yourself at home. There's only one bed, so we can share it or I can sleep on the couch. Up to you."

"I can sleep on the couch. I don't want to put you out."

"You're not. Take the bed," I tell her.

I'll just join her later, anyway. No one will be sleeping on the couch tonight.

"Okay," she says, yawning once more.

I head to my workshop; I need to work on items for the festival and also my special surprise for Kelsie.

Kelsie

I watch as Reese walks through his home and out the back door. He said he's going to his workshop. I wonder what he does? Finishing off my wine, I head into the kitchen and place my glass in the dishwasher. With the long day combined with the wine, I'm more than ready for bed.

When I reach the top step, I look around the loft, Reese's personal space. The bed is gorgeous and nothing like I've ever seen before. It's big and masculine and looks handmade from rough-hewn wood. The rest of the loft has the essentials—a wardrobe, a dresser, and a nightstand. That's it. It's minimal, but fitting for Reese. I can't see him with a bunch of clutter laying around. That's not really his style. I'll have to ask him about who made the bed, because it's fabulous. But more importantly, it looks inviting, with its fluffy down comforter and big pillows. Toeing off my shoes, I shuck my jeans and climb under the covers. It takes all of 2.5 seconds and I'm out.

Reese

I tinker in my workshop, working on a rocking horse that will be donated to the festival as part of their annual raffle. During my off hours, I like to tinker with woodworking, making kids toys and other items that people pay top dollar for.

After an hour or so, I head back inside. I don't see Kelsie or even hear a peep anywhere on the first floor, so she must be in the loft. She's probably already asleep, which is perfect because I'm ready to call it a night, too. Making my way up to my loft as quietly as possible, I shuck my clothes and get into bed, bringing Kelsie's softly snoring self into my arms. Content, I close my eyes and drift off to sleep.

* * *

The next morning, I'm awakened by Kelsie stirring in my arms. "Morning," I say in greeting.

"Morning," she says, her eyes fluttering open, her ass rubbing against my morning wood.

I have to grit my teeth to stop myself from grinding my dick against her.

"Um, I need to use the bathroom."

I let her go and she climbs out of bed, her cute little ass directly in front of me. My dick doesn't get the memo and pulses to life.

I watch as she walks across the loft and down the stairs and I have to adjust myself. As she takes care of business, I turn and lay on my back and will my dick to go down, which is no easy task. He doesn't understand that even though I had a beautiful woman in my arms last night, it does not mean he's getting action today. Sorry, buddy. Soon, very soon, I'll have Kelsie back in my bed and we won't be sleeping. But today is not the day.

Kelsie

I woke with Reese in bed with me for the second time. And he barely touched me. I thought maybe he'd make a move, but he didn't. Maybe I was wrong? Maybe he doesn't feel that way about me? If he does, he needs to make a move.

Chapter 10

Kelsie

Reese drives us back up the mountain and an awkward silence hangs between us. He showered and I just sat there, waiting to go home. It was like the awkward morning after, except nothing happened. *Again.* I look at Reese and it doesn't seem like anything is bothering him. *Well, okay then.*

Reese

As soon as I pull up to the B&B, she's out of my truck and unlocking her front door, all before I can even turn off the engine. Something has changed, but I'm not sure what that something is. So instead, I focus on getting the B&B finished. All that's left is to finish off each bathroom. The kitchen, unfortunately, will have to wait.

I get to work, when I hear the shower turn on upstairs. And that's all it takes for me to imagine Kelsie, naked and wet, to make my dick hard again. I will it to go down, but no such luck. So I think of every single unsexy thing I can think of. And after a few minutes, the water turns off and it finally goes down. Focusing on all the work that needs to get done, I start by bringing in all the furniture and putting each piece in each room, so she can bring in all her decorative stuff and get it all set up. Then, I shift my focus back to the bathrooms. I should be able to finish them by the end of next week. Which is a good thing, because her open house is coming up soon.

Kelsie

I clean up as fast as I can and begin the process of hauling everything into the B&B. There is so much stuff that Reese volunteers to help me.

"Just put everything in the foyer, for now. I need to sort everything and put it into each room."

"Yes, ma'am," he says, smiling, dimples showing.

I start going through each bag, pulling everything out, making an even bigger mess. What have I done?! Then, I get all the sheets and start them washing. I'll need them clean and ready to go so I can make all the beds. As the washer does its thing, I set about distributing everything to each bedroom. It's much more manageable that way. And just as I'm about to start decorating, I hear Abs from the foyer.

"Kels, you here?"

"Yes. Upstairs," I yell.

I hear her run up the stairs. Someone is chipper this morning.

"Well?"

"Well, what?"

"Did you?"

"Did I what?" I say, playing dumb. I know exactly what she wants to know.

"Oh, come on. Yes or no?"

I shake my head, no.

"What?!" she screeches. "You've got to be kidding me!"

"Afraid not."

"But why?"

I shrug my shoulders. I honestly don't know.

"Well, you two had better get it in gear. You're not getting any younger."

"Gee thanks, Abs."

"Just saying."

"Let's focus on this, shall we?" I say, pointing at all the stuff we bought yesterday.

Abs starts helping me take the tags off everything and placing all the items around the rooms. I hear the washer buzz and go change out laundry and come back up, continuing to decorate. By the end of the afternoon, we have all the rooms decorated and each tree set up. The place is really starting to come together. My heart grows proud of what I've accomplished. All with the help of my sister and Reese, of course. It's all starting to take shape. The Reindeer Inn is looking cozy and filled with holiday spirit.

Chapter 11

Fall has turned to Winter and Christmas is around the corner. The temps have plummeted and the skies have dropped the first snowfall of the year. I love this time of year! And speaking of this time of year... I volunteered to bring 12 dozen cookies to raise money for the annual Foxtail Ridge Christmas Festival. 12 dozen! What was I thinking?!

"No, no, no!" I growl, pulling a tray of burnt sugar cookies from the oven. Horrified, I drop the pan on the counter.

They're so burnt, I'm going to have to dump them in the trash and start over. They're so hard, a person could easily chip a tooth.

"You've got to be kidding me," I lament, Abs looking on with wide eyes. She can't believe it either. I *do not* burn anything, especially cookies. It's this old oven. It has to be.

"What are you going to do?" Abs asks me, bringing me back to the present.

"I don't know. I hope it can be fixed," I reply, feeling deflated by the minute. "I'll call Reese."

I thought the old oven worked, and it does. Sort of. It just doesn't work very well and that's a problem, not just because I need to make 12 dozen cookies in two days' time, but also because everything I will be feeding my guests will be made from scratch, just like it should be. But I can't do that if the oven doesn't work.

I hear Abs sit in one of the creaky, but lovingly restored old chairs in front of the big, brick fireplace. Pulling out my phone, I call Reese. He doesn't pick up, so I leave him a voicemail. Thinking about the stupid oven again, it makes me mad. I really can't afford a new oven right now, but I may have no choice. In the end it, there's no point obsessing over it, as the situation will work out one way or the other. There's nothing I can do to change that.

A bit defeated, I stare down at the cookies I tried to bake. They're toast. Grabbing a spatula, I scrape them out of the pan and dump them in the trash, which makes me sad and angry at the same time. I've spent so much time and energy on the place and a stupid oven is going to derail my plans. Leaning over the sink, I stare out at the snow covered mountainside, wishing it held the answers. But alas, it's stoic and cold. Same as it's always been.

I don't hear Abs walk back into the large kitchen and when she walks up and puts her arm around my shoulders, it makes me jump.

"Oh, hey Abs."

"Did you get hold of Reese?"

"I left a voicemail. I'm sure he'll get back with me soon."

Satisfied, she nods and heads out of the kitchen, leaving me alone to clean up my mess. Deciding to not even use the traitorous appliance again, I give it a mental middle finger and put the sugar cookie dough into a container with a lid, and place it in the refrigerator. At least one of my appliances still works. *For now, I snicker*. Reese will call me soon and I'll know the state of the oven once he takes a look at it.

* * *

Reese calls me later in the day and stops by to take a look at my oven.

"So what do you think is wrong with it?"

"Your thermostat is bad, from what I can tell. That's why it's overbaking your cookies."

"Can it be replaced?"

"Most thermostats can be. But this oven is pretty old. Let me check and see. If so, I can try to order the part. But it could take weeks to get in."

"Weeks! I have to have 12 dozen cookies ready by Friday," I tell him, clearly distraught. I'm not sure what I'm going to do. I look to Reese for help.

"Hey, how about you bring your supplies and use my kitchen. I have an oven you can borrow. As far as I know it works just fine."

"You don't know?"

"I rarely use it, but it's fairly new, so I would assume so."

"Are you sure?"

"Yes, I'm sure. Pack your stuff and follow me. I'll let you in."

"Thank you, Reese. I don't know how I can ever repay you."

I chuckle. "Oh, I can think of a few ways. But for now, don't worry about it. Let me have one of your cookies and we'll call it even."

She gives me a big smile. "Deal."

Reese

I help Kels pack all of her baking supplies into her SUV and follow her down the mountain to my house. Once we get there, I help her unload and bring all of her stuff into my kitchen.

"It's all yours. I need to get back to work. If you need anything, just give me a call or text. You have my number."

"Will do. And thanks again for letting me use your kitchen."

"No problem. See you later."

Walking back to my truck, I can't hide my smile. It was sheer luck that Kelsie's oven malfunctioned, because I hadn't seen her since last week, when I finished up the bathrooms at the B&B. And I wasn't sure how to make the next move. But having her in my house is a start. Now all I need is a miracle.

* * *

Later that evening, I walk into my house and the place smells like home. Kels has been baking all day and now my house smells like warm vanilla sugar cookies and spicy gingerbread men. And it makes me smile.

"Kels, you here?" I ask, when I don't see her in my kitchen. Maybe she's upstairs, in the loft?

Climbing the steps, I see her curled up in my bed, fast asleep. She looks adorable, with a little smudge of flour on her cheek and frosting in her hair. Backing away slowly, I try not to wake her, but she's a light sleeper.

"Hey, Reese. Sorry, I fell asleep. That really took it out of me," she says sleepily, yawning.

"And my oven still works?" I tease her.

"As far as I know. It works great, by the way. Oh, did you ever find out if the thermostat can be replaced in the old oven at the B&B?"

"I inquired. It's too old. You're going to need a new oven, I'm afraid."

"Bummer."

"Yep, total bummer."

"Speaking of baking, did you safe a cookie for me?" I ask, a twinkle in my eye. Kelsie's cookies are extraordinary. I should know, because I used to eat them all the time, back in the day.

"I did," she tells me, a sparkle in her eye.

"Then let's go sleepyhead. You owe me a cookie!" I tease her, throwing her over my shoulder and carrying her down the stairs.

"Was that really necessary?" she asks, more like scolding me.

I give her a smirk with dimples. "Absolutely!"

"Very well. Here, you can have these," she tells me, handing me a whole container.

"Only needed one, Kels."

"But I thought you loved my cookies!" she says, fake pouting.

"I do. And I'll certainly take all of them."

"You're welcome."

"Thank you, Kels," I say, opening the container, snagging a sugar cookie.

Taking a bite, the soft cookie melts in my mouth.

"Good?"

"The best."

"You're just saying that..."

"I'm not. They really are the best. Just wait and see. They'll be gone in no time."

"I hope so."

"I know so."

"Do you mind if I leave them here? I'll just swing by and pick them up tomorrow, on my way to the festival."

"Sure, no problem."

"Great, thanks again. I need to be going."

"Kels?" I say, stopping her before she leaves. "Be careful driving up the mountain. Text me when you get there."

"I will. Bye Reese," she says, giving me a peck on the cheek.

As soon as the door snicks shut, I grab another cookie and hatch a plan.

On Saturday, Kels rings my doorbell, ready to pick up her cookies.

"Hey, Kels."

"Hey, Reese. I'm here for the cookies."

"Sure. Let me help you load them," I tell her, taking her in from head to toe. She looks cute, in skinny jeans and boots, her blonde hair long and wavy.

We load the cookies into her SUV and then we head to the festival, since I already loaded my truck before she got here this morning.

* * *

I pull into a parking stall next to Kels. We both need to unload our stuff.

"Let me help you carry all those cookies," I say.

"That would be great. There are *so* many cookies!"

I give her a smile and open my arms wide, so she can load me up. As soon as both of our arms are full, we head to the booth we've been assigned to.

Even though it's early in the day and the Festival doesn't start until 11:00 am, everyone is in full set-up mode. There's booths up and down Main street, Christmas lights strung from above, giant foam candy canes and sugar cookies placed throughout the area. There's even a man in a Santa costume walking around. This year's festival is going to be even better than last years. And that's saying something since every year each festival is pretty damn awesome.

As we get closer to where the booths are set up, Kels asks, "What booth are we in?"

"Booth 22."

She nods and heads that direction. I just smile and follow her, cookies in tow.

"Here we are!" she announces, standing in front of booth 22.

"Yep. I'll just set these here," I tell her, gently sliding the boxes onto the fabric covered tabletop.

Kels does the same. "This looks absolutely magical. Whoever is in charge of this deserves an award."

"They sure do. I'm sure you'll be seeing members of the committee later today. They usually stop by and say hi to each booth during the festival."

"Oh, good. I'd love to meet them."

"Want to walk around? See what other booths are offering?"

"Sure! I could use a cup of hot cocoa. My hands are freezing!" she says, rubbing her hands together.

"I'm sure. Did you bring gloves?"

She pats her pockets, but comes up empty. "I did, but I must have left them in my SUV."

"Let's go get them. I need to unload my stuff anyway. But for now, let's get you warmed up," I say, taking her hands in mine, rubbing them gently, warming them with my body heat. She doesn't protest, just sighs as warmth seeps back into her hands. In no time, they're warmed up, but I don't let go of her hands.

As we walk to her SUV, almost everyone calls out a greeting to us.

"Morning Reese!"

"Hi Reese!"

"Reese, my man. Good to see you!"

Having lived here all my life, there aren't many people who don't know me. Sometimes it's a blessing, sometimes it's a curse. Small-town living at its finest. I'll introduce Kelsie later; there'll be plenty of time for that throughout the day.

When we get to her SUV, she unlocks it and grabs her gloves, slipping them on. Re-locking it, she turns to me.

"Need help carrying stuff? I can help you unload."

"That would be great," I tell her, dropping the tailgate on my truck. The stuff back here I put into boxes and the larger items, like the rocking horse, I have wrapped in a blanket. Both are pretty heavy, so I give her the rocking horse, while I grab the boxes.

"So what's in here?" she says looking down at the blanket that's in her arms. "You went out to your workshop the other day. Do you do woodworking or something?"

"I do. And what you have in your arms is a unicorn rocking horse for the raffle. It's my donation to the fundraiser."

"Oh, I can't wait to see it! Maybe we should get it back to the booth first, though."

"Probably a wise move," I reply, shutting the tailgate on my truck.

We trek back to our booth. Sitting it down gently on the table, Kels unwraps the blanket from the unicorn rocking horse and I hear her gasp, then squeal with delight. "OMG, Reese! This is amazing!"

She lovingly runs her fingers over the curves of the wood,

tracing each piece. "I can't believe you made this. Wait, yes I can! You're good with your hands!" she tells me excitedly.

Why, yes. Yes I am. Just wait until I get my hands on you, Kels.

"Thanks. It's just a hobby."

"Hobby or not, you have an amazing talent. When did you start making these?"

"A few years ago. I started small, then moved up to bigger pieces, like this one."

I see the lightbulb come on. "Your bedroom furniture. That was you."

"Yes."

"I wondered who designed it. I've never seen anything like it before."

"They're quite unique. But that's what I love about them. Chunky meets modern."

"I'd say that's pretty accurate. You have an amazing eye for detail."

I give her a smile. I'm glad she likes my work. I'm pretty proud of it myself. But you'll never hear me say that out loud.

"Ready for that hot cocoa?" I ask, noticing the food and beverage vendors are all set up.

"Yes, please!" she playfully replies.

I take her hand in mine, and lead her toward Ray's booth. He makes the best hot cocoa around.

"Hey, Ray. How are you this cold, but beautiful sunny morning?" I ask.

"Good. Going to be a busy day. How about you?"

"Very good. You remember Kelsie Marsh?"

Ray looks at Kelsie, recognition dawning. "Kelsie Marsh! Are you visiting or back for good?"

"I'm back for good. I bought the old Johnson place and Reese here has been helping me fix it up. It's now the Reindeer Inn. I'll be running it as a bed and breakfast. I'm having an open house after the first of the year. You're welcome to come."

"Well, I'll be. Good to see you're back for good. And I'll be there!" he tells her, a genuine smile on his face. Gotta love small towns.

"Two hot cocoas please, Ray."

"You got it!" he tells me, winking. The old man is a hoot.

He tinkers around and in no time, hands us two piping cups of hot cocoa, with whip cream and red and green holiday sprinkles on top.

I pull out my wallet to pay and Ray stops me. "On the house."

"Thanks, Ray."

"No problem, son. Take care of this one," he tells me, nodding at Kelsie.

"Will do."

"Thanks, Ray," Kelsie chimes, grabbing her steaming cup of hot cocoa.

I grab mine using my other hand that's not currently holding Kelsie's. I'm not letting her go.

She takes a sip and moans. "Oh, this is so good!"

I do the same, the sweet treat hitting my taste buds at warp speed. Taking another sip, I feel warmth spreading through me.

"Ready to go get set up?" I ask Kels.

"Sure. I brought a few extra, just in case."

"I wondered. I thought that wasn't exactly twelve dozen.

"Lol, more like 14."

I smile and lead her back to our booth.

We get our booth all set up and lo and behold a group of ladies are the first group to stop by. They admire my work and buy a raffle ticket, then stay and flirt with me.

"Oh, Reese. This is gorgeous. Maybe instead of spending so much time on woodworking, you could go out with me instead."

I promptly change the subject. "Have you tried Kelsie's famous sugar cookies? They melt in your mouth."

"Kelsie. As in Kelsie Marsh?"

"Yep, that's me," she tells them, her voice flat. I can tell she's annoyed.

"Just visiting, huh?" one of the ladies says from the back.

"No, actually. I'm opening a bed and breakfast in the old Johnson Place. It's called the Reindeer Inn."

"Oh, I see. Congrats. I'll take one cookie, please."

Kelsie grabs a cookie, handing it to her. The woman takes it, but doesn't take a bite.

"Well, we better move onto the next booth. Bye for now!"

As soon as she leaves, I look at Kelsie. "Sorry about that. The ladies don't seem to give up. I've never dated any of them."

She just shakes her head and takes a sip of her hot cocoa. Well, that went well. Small-town living—great for a lot of things, but not so great in other ways. Case in point: everyone knows everyone else's business. And they seem to roam in packs.

A little later, an older lady approaches us and Kelsie doesn't know she's part of the festival committee. But she will soon enough.

"Reese, my dear. Lovely to see you. And look at that beautiful unicorn rocking horse! It'll fetch a handsome sum. Thank you again for donating it."

"My pleasure, Rosie."

"And who do you have with you, dear?" she asks, like she doesn't already know. Just a few days ago, I enlisted Rosie's help. She will be pulling some mistletoe out of her pocket any minute.

"This is Kelsie Marsh," I say, pulling Kels into my side, wrapping my arm around her waist.

"Kelsie Marsh. As I live and breathe! You've come back to Foxtail Ridge?"

Kelsie smiles. "Yes, ma'am. Opening a B&B in the old Johnson Place. Now the Reindeer Inn."

"Very good," Rosie says, zeroing in on the fact that I have Kelsie tucked against me. And that's when she strikes.

"Oh! Look what I have! Mistletoe!" she exclaims, holding it up over our head.

I let out a laugh. "Rosie. You didn't."

"I did, my boy. Now you too have to kiss your lady!" she cries, a sparkle in her eye and a wide smile on her face.

I turn to Kels, smiling down at her. "You heard the lady."

Kels looks up at me and purses her lips, tilting her face toward me, bringing her lips to mine. And I take full-control. This isn't going to be some quick little peck on the lips. Nope. I turn her in my arms and bring her between my spread legs, cradling our bodies against one another, deepening the kiss. She melts into me. I swipe her lips with my tongue, demanding entrance. She opens and I swoop inside, tasting her. She tastes like chocolate and sugar cookie.

Our kiss lasts a moment too long, because I hear a polite cough from outside the booth. I pull back slightly, but keep Kels in my arms.

I'm smiling from ear to ear.

"See you later, Reese."

"Later, Rosie."

"Kels, about—"

Kels just smiles and gives me a quick peck on the lips.

Okay. That went better than I expected. Maybe there's hope for us yet.

· · ·

Once the festival is over, Kels and I pack up and head to where we parked our vehicles. There isn't much to take back home since pretty much everything sold but for a few items. Oh, and did I mention the raffle? It raised over $4,000. I'd say today was a huge success.

"Ready to go?" I ask Kels.

"Sure am. See you later?" she says, but it comes out more like a question.

I smile and pull her into my arms. "How about you follow me back to my place and we'll finish what we started."

Pink blossoms across her cheeks. And not from the cold. "I..."

"Say yes, Kels" I say, my voice deepening an octave. I'll beg if I have to.

"Okay," she replies, leaning into me, shivering.

"Cold?"

"Yes," she says, cozying up to me.

"Then let me warm you up," I tell her, grinning, my dimples dotting my cheeks. I've got a mischievous gleam in my eye, too. I can't wait to have Kels in my bed. Scratch that, she's been in my bed. I can't wait to get her naked.

She doesn't reply, just burrows deeper in my arms. Wrapping my arms around her, I hold her, resting my chin gently on the top of her head. We stay that way for several minutes, when all the sudden her tummy growls.

"Hungry?"

"Ravenous," she says, a hint of something more as she smiles at me.

"Then follow me home. I'll whip something up for us."

"And?"

"And then we can enjoy the evening. Maybe over a drink or two."

She shivers again, then gives me a quick peck on the cheek and climbs into her SUV. I walk to my truck and get in, cranking the heater. The temps keep dropping and snow is probably imminent.

I unlock the door and usher Kels inside, shrugging off my coat at the same time she does.

"Let me take your coat."

"Thank you," she says, handing it over.

I take it, along with my coat, hanging them on a peg by the door. We remove our boots while we're at it.

I see her rub her hands together, trying to warm them.

"Let me start a fire. That way you can sit by the fire and get warm while I get us a bite to eat."

"That would be amazing."

I nod and set to work getting a blazing fire started. In only a few minutes, warmth is radiating into the room, a welcome change from the frigid temps we endured for most of the day.

"There, that should help. Feel free to get underneath the blanket, if you want to."

"Yes, please," she says, grabbing the fuzzy blanket draped over the back of the couch. She lays it over her legs and tucks her arms in, getting comfy.

"How does loaded baked potato soup sound? I have some left over from the other night."

"As long as I don't have to make it, it's fine by me," she tells me, grinning.

I return her grin and head into the kitchen.

As quickly as possible, I warm up two bowls of soup and create a makeshift tray for Kels, arranging the soup, crackers, and drink on the tray. I also add a napkin and spoon. Can't forget those.

"Here we are," I say to Kels, setting the tray in her lap.

"Oh, Reese. You didn't need to do that. I could have sat at the table."

"Nonsense. Stay warm and have a bite to eat."

She looks at me pointedly. "Thank you. Where's yours?" she asks.

"It's still in the kitchen. I'll be right back."

I jog back to the kitchen and snag my soup, walking back to the great room. Carefully, I sit down in one of the chairs adjacent to where Kels is stretched out on the couch.

I see her take her first bite. "Good?" I ask her.

"Incredible. And here I thought I was the cook," she replies, smiling at me.

"I may have picked up a thing or two since you left and came back," I tell her, smiling.

"I'll say. This soup is to die for. Comfort food at its finest."

I nod, tucking into my own soup.

The rest of the meal is quiet, the crackling and popping of the wood in the fireplace the only sound between us.

"That was delicious."

"Agreed. Would you like some wine?"

"Is that a rhetorical question?" she says jokingly.

"I'll take that as a yes."

"Mmm, hmm."

"Coming right up," I tell her, lifting the makeshift tray off her lap.

Gently dropping it onto the kitchen counter, I pour us two glasses of wine.

"Here you go," I say, handing her glass to her. I keep hold of mine, watching her as she takes a sip, unreasonably jealous that her lips are touching the glass instead of touching my lips.

"Another one of your sister's leftovers?" Kels asks.

"Not this time. I may have picked up a couple bottles of wine since you were here last."

"I see. Well I, for one, am not complaining. You have impeccable taste in wine, just like so many other things."

"Oh, yeah?" I say, giving her a look. "Like what?"

She takes a healthy gulp of her wine. "Like this place, for

example. It's gorgeous, inside and out. And such an intelligent design. And the furniture; the pieces you designed and built. They're unique and stylish. Beautiful without being ostentatious. Have you ever thought about selling some of your furniture online?"

I take a drink of my wine and rub the back of my neck with my palm. "I've thought about it. But I wasn't sure anyone would be into my designs."

"OMG, Reese! I can personally say they will sell like hot cakes. Mark me!"

"I'll think about it."

She nods, her cheeks getting rosy from the warmth of the fire and the alcohol.

"All warmed up?"

"Oh, yes," she says, sticking her sock-covered toes outside the blanket, wiggling them. "I can finally feel my toes again."

"Good. Now about that kiss," I say, sitting down my now-empty wine glass on the coffee table. I get up and stalk toward her. I've waited long enough. It's time for me to claim her.

In response, she also sets her empty wine glass down on the coffee table and throws back the blanket. "What *about* that kiss?" she asks me, playing coy.

She's playing with fire.

I don't answer, instead just scoop her into my arms, planting my lips on hers. Wrapping her arms around my neck, she leans into me, returning my kiss. Never taking my lips from hers, I walk us toward my loft, then up the stairs to my bedroom.

I sit on the bed, her in my lap, as our kiss heats up. It's no longer just a kiss; it's a full-on make out session. Soon, I take it to the next level, sliding my fingers under her sweater along her ribcage. Spanning her waist, I reluctantly break our kiss.

"Kels," I say, pulling her sweater over her head, revealing she's not wearing a bra. I look my fill, then kiss my way down her neck, to her nipples. Sucking one into my mouth, I lick and suck until her back bends and her hips start to buck.

Grabbing her gently by the hips, I turn her, so that she's on her knees, straddling my hips. Meeting her eyes, I see that they're already glazed with passion.

Wanting to feel her skin on mine, I reach behind me and pull my shirt over my head, dropping it on the floor. She admires my muscles, tracing her fingers over my pecs, then between my abs, then through the trail of hair that runs southward. I sit back, giving her room to play. I don't know how long I can stay like this; my dick is hard and throbbing behind my zipper.

She traces lower, dipping into the v near my abdomen. But she's not done. She flicks open the button of my pants and delves her hand inside, gliding over the head of my dick. I shudder from the pleasure, jerking in response.

"Kels, let's get naked."

She nods and slides off my lap. Standing in front of me, she drops her jeans, but leaves her silky panties on. With her standing in front of me, I have a birds-eye view of the woman before me. I like what I see. So much so, my dick swells in my pants.

"Come here," I say, almost panting. Kels is sexy as hell.

Obeying, she steps toward me. Slipping my fingers under the band of her panties, I slide them down, revealing her inch by inch. Dropping her panties, I stand. Taking her into my arms again, I scorch her lips with a heated kiss.

Reluctantly breaking the kiss, I carefully pull down my zipper, pushing down my pants and boxer briefs and step out of my clothes. Bending down, I retrieve a condom from my pocket and sheath myself. Kels follows my every movement, watching me. We're now standing before each other, completely naked.

I take her lips once more and pull her into my arms. Taking her with me, I fall back onto the bed.

"OMG, Reese!" she exclaims, landing on top of me.

"Mmm," I say, snaking my tongue into her mouth, tasting her. I eat at her lips, all while her curves are pressed against me, making my dick throb.

Turning us over, I explore her body. I kiss her tummy, then make my way to south, licking and sucking. As I taste her, her back arches and she moans out my name.

"Reese."

Ready to be inside her, I line up the head of my dick and ease inside. She wraps her arms around my neck and her legs around my hips.

I sink into her sweet heat. "Kels," I breathe out. "You feel amazing."

"Mmm. You feel amazing, too," she murmurs, meeting my thrusts.

Taking the globes of her ass in my hands, I tilt her hips, changing the angle. She meets me thrust for thrust. I keep a steady rhythm and all too soon, I feel her orgasm, her hot breath coming in short, choppy pants as she moans out her release. The sensation is so overwhelming that it triggers my own release.

"Kels," I moan out, falling forward onto my elbows. I'm too heavy to drop on her like this.

"Mmm," she murmurs, as I kiss her neck sweetly.

Moving off her, I roll to my side, tucking her into my side.

We wake sometime later, and the snow is coming down steadily.

"How long were we out?" she asks softly.

"Almost two hours. Looks like the snow has arrived."

She bolts upright, the sheet falling to her waist. She grabs for the covers, but she's not fast enough. I get an eye full and it makes me smile. Kels has beautiful breasts. Yanking up the covers, she turns and stares out the window at the falling snow.

"Something wrong, Kels?"

"I don't think I'll be getting back to the B&B tonight."

"You're not staying?" I say, disappointed.

"I hadn't planned on it. But now..." she trails off.

"Kels, hey. The B&B will be just fine. The roads will be cleared tomorrow. I can drive you up there, if you want me to."

She looks at me. "You're right. No big deal."

Smiling, I tell her, "Exactly. Now get back under the covers."

She sighs and snuggles under the covers. I spoon her body with my own and give her hair a kiss. Closing my eyes, I revel in the fact that I have Kelsie in my arms. After this, I'm never letting her walk away again.

Chapter 13

THE WEEK BEFORE CHRISTMAS

KELSIE

The morning of the open house for the Reindeer Inn Bed and Breakfast dawns clear and bright. It's stopped snowing and the roads will be clear later today. It's perfect timing, as everyone will be here in a few hours.

Puttering down the stairs, I make my way into the giant kitchen. Looking at my new stove, I sigh. It was bound to happen, I tell myself. Opening the fridge, I set about making a simple breakfast of eggs and toast.

Filling the toaster, I press down the lever to get it started. As it toasts, I finish scrambling the eggs. That finished, I walk back to the toaster just as the lever pops up.

Perfect.

Grabbing a slice of toast with butter and jam, I place it on my plate, along with the eggs, and head into the great room. Settling in front of the fire, I enjoy one of my final peaceful mornings. Soon, I'll be opening the doors to the Reindeer Inn B&B.

A few hours later, I've scoured the place and found no more issues; everything seems to be in working order. I'm so glad Reese was able to finish up the bathrooms in time, too. I'm just concluding my walk through, when I hear Reese open and close the door.

"Kels?" he calls.

"Up here," I lightly holler. From upstairs, I walk to the landing and gaze down at him. He looks up and smiles at me, dimples dotting his cheeks.

"Hey."

"Hey."

"Ready for the open house?"

"I think so," I reply, walking down the stairs.

Nothing is malfunctioning or broken and I've got a couple dozen sugar cookies and hot cocoa, so I would say I am.

Making my way across the foyer, I step into his arms and plant a kiss on his lips. Reese returns the favor, deepening the kiss at the same time pulling me closer, fitting our bodies together.

"Mmm, I missed you," I say to him.

"Same," he says, playfully nipping at my lower lip.

And just when I think he's done, he kisses down the column of my neck, toward the open collar of my button-up shirt. Having Reese plant kisses on my skin feels marvelous. Throwing back my head, I give him better access. Not wasting time, he unbuttons my shirt and kisses the tops of my breasts. In response, my nipples pucker and my core pulses.

"Reese," I murmur.

"Mmm," he whispers, his lips against my skin.

"The door is unlocked," I say on a sigh. "Anyone could walk in at any time," I moan, almost breathless from Reese's ministrations.

He stops and looks at me, passion in his gaze. "That's the point," he says, giving me a snarky grin.

Reese is quite the tease. Who knew?

He goes back to kissing my breasts, then pulls my bra down , sucking a nipple into his mouth. I sway in his arms.

"Easy, Kels," he whispers, holding onto my hips.

As he continues to lavish attention on my nipples, I feel him walking us backwards toward the wall. Not long after, my back bumps into said wall and I'm gently pressed against it, Reese's hips grinding against me. Even with both of us wearing jeans, I can feel his arousal.

He moves back to kissing my lips and I feel him unbutton my jeans and then his own.

"Kels, I need you," he whispers.

"Not here," I whisper.

"Whatever you say, Kels," he whispers back. Then, all of the sudden, he lifts me up and carries me to my bedroom.

Once he steps into my bedroom, he shuts the door and locks it. "Better?"

"Better." And that's all the invitation he needs.

Laying me down on the bed, he strips my shirt and bra from me, then works my jeans and panties down my legs, leaving me bare.

He looks his fill, then pulls his own shirt over his head. Reese is in great shape; I can't help but stare at his abs and his happy trail leading to what's hidden behind his zipper.

Pushing down his jeans and boxer briefs, he dons a condom and crawls over me, taking my lips once again. As he kisses me, his fingers trail down my belly. Pleasuring me with his fingers, I shudder from the onslaught of pleasure. Still trembling, I feel Reese slip inside me, pushing all the way in. When he starts to move, I meet him thrust for thrust. As we move to a rhythm all our own, my release builds and I orgasm, crying out his name.

"Reese!"

In turn, his hips speed up and he thrusts in and out, rubbing me in the most deliciously of ways. Soon, he finds his own release and collapses next to me.

After a few moments, he opens his eyes and rolls over, kissing me on the lips.

* * *

Closer to 3:00 PM, people start to arrive for the open house. Of course, the first to arrive are my sister and my parents. My parents would have come sooner, but they've been out of town on a cruise. I'm glad they're back, though. I can't wait to show them what I've done with the place.

"Kelsie, dear. The place looks fabulous!" my Mom says to me.

"It really does," my Dad says, smiling.

I'm glad they like it. I'm pretty proud of it myself.

"I'm glad you approve," I tell them. "But I couldn't have done it without Abbie and Reese," I say, putting my arm around Reese's waist. Abbie just beams.

Both of my parents look at Reese and I and just smile. Like they already knew. *Of course.*

"Would you like a cookie? Or some hot cocoa? I made plenty for the open house."

"Sure thing, sweetie," my Mom says, tugging my Dad toward the table laden with cookies and hot cocoa. Abs follows behind them.

I look up at Reese and he gives me one of signature smiles, dimples on display.

"Thank you for being here," I whisper.

He kisses the top of my head. The man towers over me; always has, always will. "I'll always be here for you," he whispers back.

And my heart melts. Reese is the sweetest man.

I see the door open and close again and this time it's Reese's family who walk through the door. His sister and her husband, their kids, and Reese's parents all crowd into the foyer.

"Kelsie Marsh!" his sister exclaims. "I heard you were back. And look at this place!" she exclaims. "So this is where you've been tucked away," she teases Reese, eyeballing my arm around his waist.

He just smiles and squeezes me tighter. "Yep. And how are my favorite niece and nephew?" he says, bending down to scoop them up, hugging them tight.

"Uncle Reese! Are you gonna take us sledding?"

"Sure am!" he tells them exuberantly. "Now go get a cookie and some hot cocoa."

"Cookies and cocoa!" they scream excitedly, racing toward the table with all the goodies.

Reese turns back to me. "You like to sled, Kels?"

I blush, remembering where I was when that old memory surfaced.

"You taking me sledding, Reese Wilson?" I tease, smiling up at him.

"Yes, ma'am. On Christmas Day, my family has made it a tradition to go sledding. I'll pick you up. How does that sound?"

"I'd say that sounds amazing, I—" But I don't get to finish, when a gaggle of local single ladies step inside. And the minute I do, I know there's going to be trouble, so I paste on a smile.

"Ladies, come on in! You're welcome to look around. And there's cookies and cocoa on the table, if you're interested."

The ladies eyeball me and Reese, and one of them narrows her eyes at me. Reese, catching on quickly, wraps his arm around my waist even tighter.

"Ladies. Do enjoy a tour. Let's go, Kelsie," he says, bluntly dismissing them.

I hear them sigh and some of them huff. They're none too happy Reese is off the market. *Tough luck, ladies.*

I'm about to step away, when the door opens and in steps Rosie and Ray.

Reese pulls me toward them, never dropping his arm around my waist. "Ray! Rosie! So glad you could make it," he tells them, turning on the charm.

"Of course, my boy. Wouldn't miss it!"

I smile and invite them to look around and enjoy some cocoa. "Although my cocoa probably isn't as good as yours. But still, it's pretty darn good."

Ray just smiles and chuckles. "I'm sure it's good. But I'm here for the cookies," he jokes.

I smile as they walk away.

By the end of the day, the open house has come and gone. By my count, we had over 50 people show up today. Not too shabby. Cleaning up, I haul everything into the kitchen.

"You staying tonight?" I ask Reese.

"If you're asking, absolutely," he tells me, dropping a kiss on my lips.

"Good. Let me clean up here, then we can relax by the fire."

"Sounds good," he tells me, helping me clean up.

Reese stokes the fire and then joins me on the sofa in the great room, my back to his front.

"Mmm," I sigh. It feels good to be in his arms.

"Mmm," he murmurs back, echoing my sentiment.

"Today was a good day."

"It was."

"And I think those ladies finally took the hint."

"I sure hope so," he says, chuckling.

"Well, it's not like they have a choice," I tell him, snuggling in his arms.

"Good point," he replies, kissing me on the top of my head. I feel him lean back and get comfortable. We stay that way for the rest of the evening, snuggled up in each other's arms.

Chapter 14

CHRISTMAS DAY

KELSIE

I join my family for Christmas. We all laugh, opening gifts around the Christmas tree, a roaring fire going while Christmas music plays softly in the background. Even though we do the same thing every year, I love it. Christmas is, and always will be, my favorite holiday.

By the afternoon, we're all sleepy and our bellies are full. But this year, I won't be taking a nap after lunch, because Reese said he would pick me up and take me sledding.

So here I am, on Christmas Day, donning warm outerwear, so Reese Wilson can take me sledding again. As I pull on layer after layer, I think back to when the last time he took me sledding. And the memory makes me smile. And the thought of us making new memories also makes me smile even bigger.

I hear the doorbell and then hear Reese talking to my Dad,

wishing him a Merry Christmas. Hurrying, I grab my boots and head downstairs.

"There you are. Ready to go?" he asks me.

"Sure am! Let me get my boots on."

He nods, going back to talking with my Dad.

I get my boots on and stand up, signaling I'm ready.

"See you later, Mr. Marsh," he tells my Dad.

"Later, Reese. Take care of my daughter."

"Will do, sir."

"Ready?"

"Yes."

"Good," he replies, taking my hand in his.

"Be back later!" I announce to the entire house, heading out the door.

Reese

I take her hand and lead her out to my truck, helping her inside. I left it running so it would stay warm.

"Toasty!" she declares.

I turn and smile, backing out of her parent's driveway. Making my way up the mountain, I drop it on her.

"I've got a surprise for you, Kels," I tell her.

Her eyebrows raise in surprise. "Oh yeah?"

"Yep."

"And might I ask what this surprise is?"

I shake my head. "Then it wouldn't be a surprise, now would it."

"So I have to wait."

"'Fraid so," I say, grinning.

"Fine," she says, crossing her arms.

A few minutes later, we arrive at the same place I took her sledding when we were teenagers. But now, we're not trespassing. Parking, I shut off the engine.

"Come with me."

Kels unbuckles her seatbelt and gets out, following me to the bed of my truck. Dropping the tailgate, I pull out my surprise. "This is for you."

A custom made wooden sled with metal runners, with her name engraved into the wood, is her surprise.

"Oh, Reese. You made this for me?"

I nod.

"It's gorgeous! I love it! Thank you!" she all but shouts excitedly, hugging me.

"My pleasure. Now grab your sled and let's go!"

She grabs it and we trudge through the snow, to the exact spot I took her before. Laying down her sled, she climbs on, ready to go.

"You joining me?"

"Of course." I say, climbing on behind her.

"Here we go!" I tell her, pushing off.

It's not long and we're soaring down the mountain at breakneck speed.

We hit a bump and Kels squeals in delight, like an exuberant child.

"I love this!" she shouts.

"Me, too!"

All too soon, we have to stop or we'll crash, so I put my feet down to slow us. But I'm a little too late and we go sideways and roll. Not wanting Kelsie hurt, I wrap my arms around her and cushion her fall, my back hitting the snow, knocking the wind out my lungs.

"Oomph."

"Oh my God, Reese. Are you okay?"

I take a few deep breaths. "Just fine," I say, sitting up.

"How about you?"

"I'm perfect! That was so much fun!"

"Come here."

She scoots her bottom toward me, facing me.

I reach into my pocket and pull out a velvet box, opening it.

I turn it around and show her the ring. It's a diamond ring, with multiple diamonds in the shape of a snowflake.

"Kels, will you marry me?"

Her jaw drops. I didn't tell her about this particular surprise.

She starts to cry. "Kels?"

She blubbers. "Yes! Yes, I'll marry you!" she cries, holding out her hand. I slip the ring on her finger. It's a perfect fit.

I pull her lips to mine. "I love you."

"I love you, too."

I look deep into her eyes, all the way to her soul. "I've always loved you. You're all I ever wanted."

Epilogue

ONE YEAR LATER, CHRISTMAS DAY

REESE

I wake to a light kiss upon my lips. "Mmm, Kels, it's early," I say, my voice low and rumbly from sleep as I reach for her, bringing her into my arms.

"I have a present for you," she excitedly whispers.

My eyelids pop open. "Kels, there'll be plenty of time for that later."

She just looks at me and smiles excitedly, like she's about to burst with what she wants to tell me.

"Come here," I command, sealing her lips to mine. I lovingly kiss her until she's breathless, pink riding high on her cheeks. She wiggles in my arms, putting distance between us.

"Kels?" I ask, raising an eyebrow in question.

She doesn't answer, just takes my hand and guides it to her belly.

I'm fully awake now, my eyes wide.

"You're—?"

She nods, a huge smile on her face.

I splay my fingers over the tiny bump where our child grows. I don't even know what to say; I'm speechless. We've been trying since we got married earlier this year and it finally happened. Kelsie's given me the best present, well, ever. Not sure if she'll ever be able to top this one. And I'm not sure I want her to.

My eyes go in search of hers and she has a look of utter happiness on her face. I happily mirror her look, tipping her head toward mine, taking her lips once again. I kiss her tenderly, until we're both breathless. Gently rolling her onto her back, I kiss every inch of her gorgeous body, then make sweet love to my gorgeous wife, thanking my lucky stars that she's mine. She's all I ever wanted.

If you enjoyed Kelsie's story, grab a copy of Abbie's story, All I Ever Needed today!

All I Ever Needed
All I Ever Book 2

Abbie

Stepping inside Sam's Place, I look around for Matt, spotting him in a booth near the back. As I walk to the booth, I reach for my gloves, peeling them off. I notice Matt watches me the entire time, his gaze never leaving me, even as I rid myself of my coat.

"Glad you made it," he says, his lips twitching a bit. "I thought you might not show."

I snort. "I said I would, so here I am," I reply sarcastically, sliding into the booth. "You trying to dig yourself a deeper hole?" I ask.

He shakes his head.

I smirk. It's going to make more than flowers to change my mind.

Settling in, the waitress approaches and drops off menus and takes our drink orders.

"Water to start," I say.

"Same," Matt says.

The waitress nods and heads off towards the bar.

"So what's good here?" Matt asks.

"Pretty much everything. I'm partial to the spicy black bean burger."

He quirks an eyebrow. You don't eat meat?"

"Nope. Vegetarian for life."

"I see. Is it okay to eat it with you?" he asks, innocently.

I lightly laugh. "You're joking."

"Um, no. Just checking."

"Of course, silly. Order whatever you like."

He looks relieved. "Then cheeseburger and fries, it is."

We close our menus and lay them down, signaling the waitress. She approaches and takes our order. And this time, I go for a beer.

"And an IPA, please. Want anything?" I ask Matt. "I recommend anything locally brewed."

Snapping open his menu again, he takes a look at the beer selections. "I'll have a milk stout nitro."

The waitress nods and takes our menus. The moment she leaves, I can't but help tease Matt a little bit.

"Black coffee and now dark beer. Is there something you want to tell me," I joke. "You know what they say about black coffee: only psychopaths drink coffee black."

He shrugs. "Nope. And speaking of coffee, you took mine."

"You don't say," I joke, laughing lightly.

"That's a serious offense."

"Oh, really?" I tease.

"Yes," he deadpans, faking indignation.

"From where I'm sitting, you deserved it."

He shakes his head and smiles. "Touché."

The waitress drops off our beer. I take a sip, watching Matt as he does the same.

"Well?" I inquire.

I watch as he swallows, his throat working with the movement. Gah, even Matt makes drinking look sexy. Who knew?

"Damn, that's good," he replies, savoring the notes.

I smile. "Local brews reign supreme."

"No complaints here," he says, holding up his pint. "Here's to starting over. Cheers!"

I mirror his actions. "To starting over," I say. I should probably lay off a bit when it comes to teasing Matt. He really isn't that bad. And he is trying.

Matt

We both take a sip of our beer and wait for our food to arrive.

"Mandy tells me you grew up here."

"I did."

"Never wanted to leave?"

"Kelsie, my sister, did the leaving. She only recently moved back here from Denver."

"I see. What does she do?" I ask.

"She runs the Reindeer Inn Bed & Breakfast."

"Sounds cozy. Is it open?" I inquire.

"Not yet, but soon though. I've been helping her rehab the place. She's been crazy busy with getting ready for the B&B opening while also planning her wedding."

"Gotcha. And do your parents live here?"

"They do. Been married almost forty years."

"Wow, that's a long time."

"Well, we Marsh's take our time and only marry for love. Love that will last a lifetime."

"Not a bad thing."

"Nope. And take my sister and her husband Reese, for example. He's been in love with her since high school, but was too nervous to tell her. Which is crazy, because that's not like

Reese at all. Then she left for Denver. He was miserable until she came back a few months ago. Yours truly played matchmaker. And the rest, as they say, is history."

"Nice little story. Is everything fairytale-like up here?"

She laughs. "Maybe? I don't know. There is most definitely something about Foxtail Ridge, though. The love stories are epic," she says on a sigh.

Then it gets me thinking. Abbie isn't attached, is she?

"And what about you, Mr. Ellis?"

"For the love of God, woman, call me Matt. Whenever you call me Mr. Ellis, I have to stop myself from looking around for my father," I tell her, laughing and shaking my head. No one calls me that. Except for her.

"Okay, Matt," she says, putting stress on the vowel. "What about you? No girlfriend or wife? I don't see a ring."

"Single as can be. Thus, no ring," I tell her looking down and wiggling my bare ring finger on my left hand. Interesting that she would mention that. Maybe she's—

"Any family?" she asks, interrupting my thoughts, as she lobs questions in rapid succession.

"My parents still live back East. My brother lives on the West Coast." That's enough with the questions, I think to myself. Time to turn the tables.

"And how about you, Abbie? No boyfriend or husband?

"Nope. Single, too."

I nod. It makes me hopeful, because I would really like to stick around and see where this goes.

Not long after, the waitress drops off our burgers and we tuck into our food. We eat, we chat some more about random things, we laugh, and we get to know each other. By the time our food and beer is gone, we're on better terms. And I aim to keep it that way.

The waitress returns, dropping the bill onto the table. "I've got this," I say, placing my card in the tray.

"Thank you. Dinner's on me next time."

I nod, agreeing. That's the best thing I've heard all day. Next time. Note to self: better cancel your flight. I can't wait to see Abbie again.

Grab a copy of All I Ever Needed today!
www.stacykristenauthor.com

About Stacy Kristen

Stacy Kristen is an indie author who writes erotic romance and romantic suspense novellas with HEAs for those who just want a short, steamy read. She's an avid reader of romance and enjoys baking, drinking lots of caffeine, traveling, and laughing with the squirrels in her backyard.

https://www.stacykristenauthor.com/

Books by Stacy Kristen

www.stacykristenauthor.com

Single Titles

Love Under Construction: Part One & Part Two

Moto Luvin'

All About Her

Snow One But You

Only One for Me

Sweet As Puck

Forever & Always

Worth Waiting For

Naughty Neighbor

Replete In My Duty (Piper Falls Station 28)

Desert Aces MC

Vegas Redemption (Set in the world of Desert Aces MC)

Desert Aces MC: Jamie (Book 1)

Desert Aces MC: Jax (Book 2)

Desert Aces MC: Mac (Book 3)

Box Set

Coveted Duet

Coveted by the Billionaire (Coveted Book 1)

Coveted by the Captain (Coveted Book 2)

Box Set

<u>*Anthology*</u>.

Be Mine: A Collection of Short & Steamy Romances

<u>*All I Ever Duet*</u>

All I Ever Wanted (Book 1)

All I Ever Needed (Book 2)

All I Ever Box Set

<u>*St. James Security*</u>

When Trouble Finds You (Book 1)

When Danger Follows You (Book 2)

Collateral Damage (Book 3)

St. James Security Box Set

<u>*Damiani Crime Family*</u>

Cunning Heir (Book 1)

Newsletter Sign-Up

Sign-up for my newsletter for the latest information, new releases, and freebies!

Newsletter Sign-Up

www.ingramcontent.com/pod-product-compliance
Lightning Source LLC
Chambersburg PA
CBHW051127160726
47997CB00018B/811